WHAT OTHERS ARE SAYING...

Who would think of creating fairy tales from a Deaf-centric perspective? Only the brilliant and talented Roz Rosen can put together her version of the old classics. These stories are not just for deaf children—they serve as a great learning tool for all children of all ages. Readers can revisit these familiar tales and view them with fresh eyes and appreciation.

Linda Bove, Actress

Finally! A Deaf-centric reframe on our treasured fairy tales that will surely breathe new life into these ageless classics.

Flavia S. Fleischer, Ph.D., California State University, Northridge Deaf Studies Department Chair

Whether you are a child or an adult, whether you are Deaf or not, this book by Roz Rosen will definitely enrich your perception of Deaf people. The fairy tales offer an excellent opportunity for classroom discussion of the self-image of Deaf people and the issues that concern them most in their daily interactions with the hearing world. The book also lends itself to storytelling in American Sign Language—a great potential for dramatization on stage or screen.

Bernard Bragg, National Theatre of the Deaf Co-founder

For a culture so rich, encompassing and profound there is a surprising shortage of literature that speaks directly to deaf people. Roz Rosen's stories fill a void in that regard; her spins on familiar classics are enriching, hilarious and empowering.

They are a valuable, lasting addition to a canon that will only expand in the years to come, thanks to trailblazing authors like Roz.

David Kurs, Deaf West Theatre Artistic Director

Deaf Culture Fairy Tales, authored by Roslyn Rosen, a well-known educator of deaf children, is a collection of well-known children's fairy tales that have been adapted for reading and telling in American Sign Language. The use of American Sign Language as a language base to further develop a second language, such as English, has long been verified by examination and experience, but adapting reading materials has not kept pace. This book breaks new ground and will be a welcome addition to any home or school library as well as Deaf Studies programs and teacher preparation programs.

Robert R. Davila, Ph.D., Gallaudet University President Emertius

As a passionate literacy advocate for young children, what a joy to see more angles of familiar stories by brilliantly incorporating Deaf culture and capitalizing on signers' ways of communicating. These adapted stories provide an education for all, passing on the joy of reading for many more generations to come!

Deanne Bray, Actress and Teacher

These stories are beloved classics with a Deaf-centric twist, making them innovative, entertaining, and educational. With the growing interest in American Sign Language, these stories add wonderful opportunities for parents and children to learn and create new memories together. These adapted stories are also part of a growing and vital corpus of literature supporting bilingual approaches towards language literacy.

Roberta "Bobbi" Cordano, J.D., Gallaudet University President

Deaf Culture Fairy Tales

By Roz Rosen

Illustrated by Yiqiao Wang

First Edition, January 2017

Written by Roslyn "Roz" Rosen

Illustrated by Yiqiao Wang

Published by Savory Words Publishing
www.savorywords.com

ISBN 978-0-9863552-6-4

Printed in the United States of America

To my wonderful parents and first teachers,
Ruth Katzen and Abe Goodstein

and

My beloved family: my husband Herb,
and our children, Jeff, Steve, and Suzy

TABLE OF CONTENTS

FOREWORD

"As long as we have deaf people on earth, we will have signs. It is my hope that we will all love and guard our beautiful sign language as the noblest gift God has given to deaf people."

George Veditz

What is the tallest building in the world? As everyone knows, that's the library with its millions of stories. As a Deaf child growing up in New York City in the days before captioned television, I was fortunate to have Deaf parents who read to me and my brother, Harvey, in sign language making the stories in static, staid books leap to life. As soon as I could read by myself, my parents gave me a library card, one of my most cherished gifts. I started going to the city library every weekend to borrow armfuls of books that I devoured.

I especially loved the classics, adventure stories, and fairy tales. Books were my friends. However, there was a disconnection: none was about my people or my community or my language. Nothing about our way of life, our experiences, our culture, or our ability to navigate and to create solutions for ourselves in a multifaceted, multicultural society.

What if Snow White or Cinderella were Deaf? Would they still get the prince? What if the Big Bad Wolf had simply been Deaf? With the infusion of the Deaf experience, would the stories take a different turn? What if, with a dash of magic, everyone could converse in sign language? The possibilities were endless—thus, this book was conceived.

Deaf Culture Fairy Tales is a book written for kids of all ages and people, Deaf or hearing, from all walks of life. It is a book designed to entertain, captivate, and introduce readers and storytellers to different ways of living and loving.

American Sign Language (ASL) is an authentic language in and of itself, meeting all standards of a robust language with its own grammar, syntax and rhythm. ASL is also deeply embedded in the Deaf community and its culture. Distinct from English, ASL is expressed through three-dimensional hand movements, and is nuanced with facial expressions and placement on the body. Some of the songs within these stories are capitalized, indicating ASL gloss; this indicates they are intended to be signed, often with a repetitive handshape and a rhythmic beat.

This collection has been adapted with Deaf characters and Deaf experiences. However, "The Phoenix," a story about a mythical bird, weaves and links actual milestones in Deaf history into a story-like series of positive accomplishments.

I am delighted that my daughter Suzy rose up to my challenge of contributing a story to this collection. The result is her enchanted version of "The Tortoise and the Hare," reflecting her immersion in the Deaf community and her love of technology.

In addition to my husband and family whose endless well of support enabled me to write this book, I want to thank Yiqiao Wang, who enchanted the book with her marvelous illustrations, and the T.S. Writing Services team, who served as my editor and publisher patiently working with me, stitching together my stories with a magical thread and needle into a coherent whole. I hope you have as much fun reading this book as I did writing it.

My appreciation and admiration also go to our Deaf community, with its boundless heritage and linkages.

Roz Rosen
January 2017

LITTLE RED RIDING HOOD

ittle Red Riding Hood, so named because of the red hood and cape she loved to wear, arrived home from school. Her house smelled wonderful; her mother had been baking breads and canning jam. She made a beeline to the kitchen, tapped her mom, and said, "I'm home!"

Her mother hugged her and signed, "It's time for you to take this basket of freshly baked breads and jam to Grandma." Grandma lived by herself in the woods, and she had not felt well lately.

"Now," her mother admonished, "as always, stay on the path and do not talk to strangers. Come right back."

"I know, I know," signed Little Red Riding Hood, tapping her fingers on her temple. "I'll go now." She picked up the basket and started on her way.

Mom shouted out of the doorway, "Little Red Riding Hood!"

It sounded like "Lit Riddle Hod" but Little Red Riding Hood knew it was her mom calling her name. She stopped in her tracks, turned around and looked at Mom.

Mom signed, "Love you. Thanks for your help," and blew a kiss.

Her mom was Deaf and just wonderful! Grandma was also Deaf. Little Red Riding Hood felt proud that she was both a Kid of Deaf Adults (KODA) and a Grandkid of Deaf Adults (GODA). She felt she had special skills that the other kids didn't have; she was fluent in sign language. Sometimes when spoken words failed her, she would clarify with a sign or gesture. Or she would emphasize a point with her hands, making the point more effective.

The path to Grandma's house wound through the woods, passing small areas of grassy meadows, meandering through clusters of flowers and blueberries, and crossing over bubbling brooks. Little Red Riding Hood enjoyed the walk, especially after being inside at school all day. She was thinking of the homework for her language class: writing a paper. She thought maybe the benefits of bilingualism would be a good topic.

Little Red Riding Hood was lost in her thoughts as she walked along the path. Big Bad Wolf spied her walking alone. He could smell the bread in her basket. But Little Red Riding Hood would be even more delicious! He would follow her and figure out where she was going. When Little Red Riding Hood came to a fork in the path and turned right, Big Bad Wolf knew that she was headed for her grandma's house. He could race ahead and trap her in the house.

Big Bad Wolf arrived at the house, and saw Grandma in bed. She had on a nightgown, a nightcap, and spectacles. He pounced on Grandma and swallowed her. He then put on Grandma's nightcap and spectacles, got into bed, and pulled the quilt up to his chin. "It won't be too long now before Little Red Riding Hood arrives," chuckled Big Bad Wolf as he licked his chops.

Shortly, the lights flickered, signaling that Little Red Riding Hood had pressed the doorbell. The front door opened, and in waltzed Little Red Riding Hood. She went directly to Grandma's bed and showed Grandma her basket of goodies.

She looked at Big Bad Wolf and signed, "What big eyes you have!"

Big Bad Wolf was amazed at the fact he could understand Little Red Riding Hood's signs. He had not seen sign language before but there seemed to be some connection. Maybe it was just because Little Red Riding Hood looked so delicious.

But Big Bad Wolf merely nodded in response.

"What big ears you have!"

Again, Big Bad Wolf merely nodded.

Little Red Riding Hood was becoming concerned, because it was not typical for Grandma to just nod. Grandma always loved to chat with Little Red Riding Hood.

"What big teeth you have!"

"Grgrugrrr," gurgled Big Bad Wolf, drooling in anticipation of eating her up. He jumped out of bed and tried to grab Little Red Riding Hood.

But Little Red Riding Hood held out her palm and stopped him. She signed, "Are you Deaf? You sound different from the other wolves."

"Me, Deaf?!" thought Big Bad Wolf, "aha, that's it."

Just then, a woodsman passing by looked in the window and saw Little Red Riding Hood and Big Bad Wolf towering over the little girl. It looked like he was ready to pounce on her. The woodsman took out his axe, burst into the house, and ran towards Big Bad Wolf.

Big Bad Wolf loosened his eye-lock on Little Red Riding Hood, quickly jerked away, and his violent body movement caused Grandma to pop out through his mouth.

The woodsman shouted at the top of his lungs, "I'll save you both." He started to swing his axe at Big Bad Wolf.

"Stop!" signed Grandma.

"Stop!" yelled Little Red Riding Hood.

The woodsman, with his axe raised and aimed at the wolf, was startled. His arm froze in mid-air, as he wondered what in tarnation was going on.

Little Red Riding Hood and Grandma grabbed the woodsman's axe and threatened to chop him up into little pieces if he did not stop meddling in other people's business, and ordered him to leave their house immediately.

"The nerve of the woodsman! We Deaf people and KODAs can make our own decisions and take care of ourselves." They looked at Big Bad Wolf, who didn't seem so menacing anymore.

Big Bad Wolf stared back at them, trying to figure out what just happened. Grandma signed, "You're Deaf like me. We will teach you sign language. You, like most Deaf creatures, will catch on quickly. We can be friends. Now let's have some tea and enjoy the bread and jam. Come, sit down at the table with us."

As they clicked their teacups, they happily sign-chanted with Big Bad Wolf clumsily following along, "Nothing about us without us!"

THE UGLY DUCKLING

ucks of different hues and shades were swimming around a lake. Spring was in the air, and blossoms decorated trees with splashes of color. Daffodils and dandelions dotted the landscape in bursts of yellow. Animals around the lake greeted each other like long-time friends as they came out of hibernation. Springtime always brought happy new beginnings and celebrations. Baby ducklings were hatching, and flocks of ducks paddled from nest to nest, viewing all the ducklings. They admired and complimented themselves on such beautiful babies. The baby ducklings quacked softly and basked in all that attention. Often their cooing was rewarded with delicious insects and tiny fish brought by the visitors.

One nest of ducklings included one duckling different from the others; visiting ducks stared at it in pity. It had one brown eye and one blue eye. Its feathers were grey instead of yellow, and its bill was black instead of orange. Everyone felt sorry for Mother Duck's misfortune of having such an ugly baby. When the ducklings quacked, the ugly duckling simply opened his bill and gurgled. "What's wrong? It doesn't sound like the other ducklings," the visitors thought. "What an ugly duckling," one duck whispered. The name stuck, much to Mother Duck's dismay.

Mother Duck tried to shield her baby from those comments, but Ugly Duckling's feelings were hurt. She told Ugly Duckling, "Do not pay attention to them. You are as good as your brothers and sisters. You do look and sound different, but it doesn't matter. I will invite Dr. Karl Quack to examine you."

Dr. Karl Quack was revered as a wise physician with years and years of experience. He examined Ugly Duckling, poking him and peering at his eyes, nose, throat, ears, feet, and tail. He lifted Ugly Duckling and held him upside down and then held him this way and that way. Finally, Dr. Quack announced his verdict: "Bad news. He is Deaf."

"Deaf?!" exclaimed Mother Duck. "Is there no hope?"

The doctor responded, "Well, I do have good news. We offer excellent listening and speaking therapy and ointments. With our exclusive therapy, as well as in grooming, your baby will outgrow his deafness and ugliness, and be just like you." Mother Duck's heart jumped with joy and relief at this wonderful news.

Ugly Duckling started daily lessons with Dr. Quack's certified and qualified speech and grooming therapist. Ugly Duckling did not like those lessons because he wanted to be with the other ducklings and to play with them. "Mom," he said, "the lessons aren't helping. Let's stop them."

"Oh, baby," answered Mother Duck, "your speech and looks are slowly but surely improving."

"No, they're not," retorted Ugly Duckling, "you're just getting used to the way I talk and look."

After a few weeks, Ugly Duckling's speech and looks had not improved very much. Mother Duck asked Dr. Quack to come back to re-examine Ugly Duckling. Maybe there was something else that could be done. Dr. Quack examined Ugly Duckling again, poking him and peering at his eyes, nose, throat, ears, feet, and tail. He lifted Ugly Duckling and held him upside down and then held him this way and that way. Finally Dr. Quack stated that the excessive flapping of wings stunted his speech development. The remedy was to fasten a rubber belt around Ugly Duckling's body so that his wings could not move. Luckily, Dr. Quack was having a sale on these rubber belts, and Mother Duck gratefully bought one.

Ugly Duckling hated the rubber belt because he could not move his wings. He could no longer use his wings to help him communicate his wants and needs. He could no longer use his wings to help him move faster, navigate through the tall marsh grasses, or learn to fly like the other ducks. He could only waddle on land or paddle his feet in water. He could not even defend himself from the other jeering fowl. Even Mother Duck got tired of protecting Ugly Duckling and began ignoring him most of the time. She was embarrassed that Ugly Duckling was part of her brood.

Ugly Duckling was miserable, but he continued with his speech and grooming lessons. He hoped that he would improve enough that the despicable rubber belt would be removed and that his mother would start paying attention to him again.

Days and weeks passed. It was now late summer. The cattails grew tall. Water lilies started to fade away. The foliage on the trees around the lake transformed into an artist's palette of brilliant yellows, oranges, and reds.

Even after all those daily lessons, Ugly Duckling still sounded and looked different from the other ducks. His neck had grown long and curvy. Dr. Karl Quack had said that speech lessons might elongate the neck and that was perfectly normal; his neck would shrink back once he mastered perfect quacking. His fuzzy feathers had fallen out and his new grey feathers looked different from those of the other ducks. He was a different shape and color from the other ducks. Dr. Quack explained that this was all simply part of the process and that Ugly Duckling had to continue with his speech and grooming lessons.

Ugly Duckling was now bigger than all of his brothers and sisters. While they tolerated their ugly sibling, they did not want to take him along with them when playing with their friends. He looked and sounded strange, and was the brunt of their jokes. They hissed at him, hit him, or bit him. Even though Ugly Duckling was bigger than all the ducks, he was scared of them. Ugly Duckling, always lonely, often went off by himself near the grassy marshes and pretended he was invisible. He watched the ducks fly and wished he could get rid of his rubber belt so he could soar like them.

Different flocks of birds stopped at the lake on their various migration routes. One flock had brown birds with long striped necks and big wings, and they hissed. The geese looked at Ugly Duckling and laughed at him. He certainly was a sorry sight, with a rubber belt around him. They taunted him and then they flew away.

Bang, bang!

Shots rang out, hitting two of them. Dogs dove into the lake to bring the downed geese back to the hunters. The dogs saw Ugly Duckling but swam right past him to recover the downed geese. Ugly Duckling was terrified and paddled away as fast away as he could, as far away as he could, to his secret hiding place in the grassy marshes near the edge of the lake. He stayed as still as he could, peering over the marshes, watching in all directions to make sure he was safe.

The days grew shorter. The nights grew colder. Trees shed all their leaves. Ugly Duckling's mother, brothers, and sisters had already flown south, leaving Ugly Duckling behind. Mother Duck said that Ugly Duckling had to stay in that lake in order to continue with his speech and grooming lessons. But the speech and grooming therapist had migrated south with the flock of ducks! "Maybe another therapist will come soon," Ugly Duckling hoped.

White fluff started to fall from the sky. Ugly Duckling had never seen snow before, and he marveled at how beautiful and pure the snow made everything look. He paddled around the lake to look around. He noticed that the snow on the lake formed a blanket of ice and that he could not paddle through the ice. As the days passed, the ice blanket on the lake grew larger and deeper. The area for Ugly Duckling to paddle around in grew smaller and smaller.

One evening, Ugly Duckling fell asleep in the marsh grasses near the edge of the lake. The sunrise the next morning awakened

him, and he set forth on his daily forage for food. But he could not move! He realized that ice had formed all around him and he was now stuck in the ice! He decided to wait a bit longer; maybe the ice would go away. He had noticed that the sun warmed the water and melted the snow on the branches and in the marshes. The day passed, and Ugly Duckling was still stuck in the ice. He paddled his feet underneath, hoping that he could somehow break loose. He twisted his body this way and that way, but was as stuck as ever. Gradually, ice started to cover his body.

Ugly Duckling was hungry and petrified. What would happen to him? A couple more days passed. He craned his neck, peering around the tops of the brown frozen marshes, watching for help or any possible menaces. One day, an old man and his cat were walking nearby, gathering sticks for a fire. Ugly Duckling saw them approaching and quickly ducked his head back into the cattails. But Cat had already seen him, and came towards him, followed by the old man.

They saw him, stuck in the ice. The old man took out his axe. "Oh no, this is the end of me," thought Ugly Duckling. He tried to hide his head under his wing, but it was impossible, with the ice and the rubber belt. The axe swung, not at him but at the ice around him, again and again, until Ugly Duckling was freed! The old man then swung at him, but gently, to break up most of the ice that had enveloped his body.

The old man looked at him. "What a sorry sight you are! Why are you still here instead of in the south?" he asked.

Ugly Duckling gurgled with joy at being freed, but he still shook with fear. What would the old man do with him? He had seen many ducks and geese killed by men like him.

"Come, follow me home and get thawed out near our fireplace," the old man beckoned at Ugly Duckling. Ugly Duckling was uncertain what to do, but whatever happened was better than being frozen and unable to move. The old man trudged through the pristine snow, leaving behind footprints. Cat leaped from one footprint to the next footprint, closely following the old man. Ugly Duckling waddled behind Cat on the top of the unbroken snow crust. They inched towards the old man's house and finally arrived home.

Ugly Duckling had never seen a house, let alone been in one. The old man's wife welcomed them all, removed the old man's coat, and rubbed the wet cat down. She encouraged Ugly Duckling to sit near the fireplace to thaw. After he became warm and dry, the old couple saw the rubber belt around Ugly Duckling's middle. The strange device made Cat's fur stand on end and his tail thrice as big. The farmer and his wife's mouths fell open. Ugly Duckling was startled and scared by their reaction.

"What is that?!" asked the old man.

"I don't know but let's remove it," replied his wife.

"No, no," shrieked Ugly Duckling, "I need it to help improve my speech." To protect his belt, he bolted away from the old man, his wife and the cat, and hid in a deep nook between cabinets, out of their reach.

But of course the old man and his wife could not understand what Ugly Duckling said. "Okay, have it your way," said the wife. "Settle down and have some grub."

Ugly Duckling felt safe and comfortable in this house. He was warm, and enjoyed his daily ear of corn. He was free to move around in the house and could go outside on sunny days to play with Cat. He liked Cat although sometimes the cat scared him by pouncing on him or by grabbing his ear of corn. But Cat was his only friend, and they had a special kinship. They could understand each other through facial expressions and gesturing with their heads, bodies or feet.

Cat asked, "What are you?"

Ugly Duckling replied, "I'm a duck."

"Duck? I've never seen a duck like you."

"Yes, I know. Everyone calls me Ugly Duckling and everyone except you hates me."

"Why do you keep that belt on?"

"Because my mom and my speech therapist said it will make me speak better and become beautiful."

Cat was incredulous. He could not understand why Ugly Duckling preferred to talk and to be pretty than to do what ducks naturally do. "Speak better?! Become beautiful? Of what use are these if you cannot be yourself? Ducks don't speak. Ducks don't need to be beautiful."

He thought further and added, "And ducks fly. You can't."

"Yes, I know," Ugly Duckling said. "But when I talk pretty and look pretty, they will remove the belt and then I can learn to fly. And then everyone will like me."

"Who knows about that? What if that doesn't happen? Not only will you still be ugly and unable to talk, but also unable to fly," Cat said.

Ugly Duckling shrugged, but struggled to keep tears from rolling down his cheeks. "It's what Mother Duck wants. I want to make her proud of me."

Cat stared at Ugly Duckling. "You do know that you are Deaf?"

"Deaf?" responded Ugly Duckling. "How do you know?"

"I'm Deaf, too. That's why we can connect and communicate with each other."

Ugly Duckling was floored. "So that's why you're the only one who can understand me. How is that possible?"

"We Deaf creatures have intuition that alerts us to whether another creature is Deaf, too. We can tell by their eyes and expressions. We always can connect and communicate easily."

"Really?" Ugly Duckling was beginning to feel a glimmer of hope.

"Yes, really. We lived in the city before the old man retired and moved out here. There were tribes of cats in different neighborhoods in the city. Some were Italian, some were French, some were Spanish, and some were African. But we could understand, connect and communicate easily with each other. We often got together at night under street lights."

"What an amazing skill to have!" murmured Ugly Duckling. "Maybe someday I will meet them."

The frigid days of winter passed by. Ugly Duckling grew bigger and bigger. His rubber belt got more and more snug. One day the rubber belt snapped!

"Oh dear me," he bemoaned. "Mother Duck will be so unhappy with me. Dr. Quack will be so furious with me."

He struggled to put the belt back on, but it was useless. His wings, stiff from non-use, could not help. He tried to put the belt around his neck, but it kept slipping off.

Ugly Duckling pleaded with Cat, "Look, my belt is broken. Please put it back on me. Maybe you can add a string to it?"

Cat was sitting on the fireplace mantle with a smug look on his face. He had been watching Ugly Duckling struggling. "No way," Cat said as he shook his head. "Now you can learn to be yourself. You can learn to like yourself just as you are."

Tears rolled down Ugly Duckling's cheeks. All his hopes to talk clearly and to be attractive were dashed. His life would have no purpose now.

The next day was sunny, and Cat told Ugly Duckling to come outside to play with him. The ground was still cold and the trees were still barren, but tiny buds had started appearing here and there.

"Come, let's have a race," said Cat to the forlorn Ugly Duckling, "I'll race you to that tree." Ugly Duckling grudgingly agreed.

Both yelped and ran as fast as they could, and Cat won handily as Ugly Duckling came waddling, huffing and puffing all the way.

"Now," said Cat, "try flapping your wings as you run. You will go faster."

Ugly Duckling slowly lifted his wings, and winced with pain as he stretched his wing muscles. They had been belted down for so long they were almost useless.

"Wider! Higher!" coached Cat.

Snap, crackle, and pop! Ugly Duckling's wing muscles creaked as he stretched them wider and higher. He was amazed at his wing span and how good it felt to open up all the way.

After a few days of practice, Ugly Duckling could keep pace with Cat by flapping his wings as he raced to the finish line. He also discovered that he could use his wings to communicate even better with Cat.

One day as they were racing, Ugly Duckling felt a lift and realized he was actually flying short distances. His formerly useless wings had become stronger and stronger. He loved to race Cat and looked forward to beating Cat someday soon.

Another day, Ugly Duckling saw Cat perched on a tree limb above him.

"Come down. I'll race you to the tree at the edge of the lake," said Ugly Duckling.

"Not until you sit on this limb next to me," replied Cat.

"But that's impossible!" said Ugly Duckling.

"Where there is a will, there is a way. You want to race? Get up here first," cajoled Cat.

Ugly Duckling flapped his wings but could not lift himself high enough to reach the limb. Cat suggested that he combine running with flapping. Ugly Duckling thought about that suggestion, and decided to try it. He waddled ten feet away from the tree, started running and flapping his wings. Although that gave him a higher lift, it was not sufficient to reach the limb. So he backed up fifty feet from the tree and tried again. It was still not sufficient to reach the limb.

He went a hundred feet away from the tree and made a running start, flapping his wings even harder. To his amazement, he soared higher and higher and reached the limb where Cat was! He tried to land on the limb but found that he could not hold on. His webbed feet were not made to climb on trees or to hang on limbs. Ugly Duckling wobbled on the limb and finally fell off the limb.

"Flap your wings! You can fly now!" implored Cat.

That statement hit Ugly Duckling like a bolt of lightning. "I can fly? Oh, I can fly!" He quickly flapped his wings just as he was about to hit the ground. He soared upwards and then in large, loping circles above the meadow, and swooped down and back up again, before gently landing on the ground. The feeling was exhilarating! It seemed like the most natural thing to do. Yes, finally he was doing what he was born to do!

"That is who you are!" said Cat.

"Thank you, Cat!" said Ugly Duckling.

Spring soon sprung. Flowers and leaves appeared on cherry and apple trees. Tulips and hyacinths peered through the ground. The ice on the lake was mostly thawed. The old man and his wife said it was time to plant seeds. They moved slowly but were determined to maintain their daily routines. Ugly Duckling noticed that white hairs like the ones on the old couple's heads had sprouted on Cat's face. Ugly Duckling noticed with some alarm that a few of his new feathers on his wings were white, like the hair of the old man and his wife and like the white hairs on Cat's face. "I must be getting old now," thought Ugly Duckling.

Being near the lake reminded Ugly Duckling of his happy days of yore, paddling around. He loved paddling around; that too was what ducks were born to do. He tiptoed into the water and was relieved he still remembered how to swim. "Come on," he beckoned Cat, "the water is fine."

Cat arched his back and his tail grew three times as large. "Never! It's not what cats do," he hissed. Seeing the look of disappointment on Ugly Duckling's face, Cat said gently, "It's fine for you to be you and for me to be me. Be proud of yourself."

Ugly Duckling pondered Cat's statement. He reflected on how they first found him, frozen, hungry, and terrified, several months ago. He remembered how miserable he had been then, feeling as if he could not do anything right. He realized that he had learned and grown a lot just by doing what he could do best: swimming, flying, and communicating with his wings.

A few days later, Ugly Duckling saw different flocks of birds migrating north, and landing around the lake to rest. He decided it was time to search for his family; they probably had returned to the lake, too.

He bid the old man, his wife and Cat a tearful farewell, thanked them profusely for all they did for him, and encouraged them to visit him at the lake sometime.

Ugly Duckling waddled over to the lake and paddled to a distant lagoon where his family lived. He noticed different flocks of birds in the lake. Some flocks had large birds, others had small birds. Some flocks had striped birds, and others were brown birds with colorful strands of feathers. There was one flock of large white birds.

Ugly Duckling finally arrived at the lagoon and found his family.

"Mother Duck, Mother Duck, I've found you!" exclaimed Ugly Duckling.

Mother Duck looked up at him and said, "Go away, you don't belong here."

"Don't you remember me?" pleaded Ugly Duckling, his squeaky little voice breaking. He hoped she would understand him after all his speech lessons.

Mother Duck, his sisters and brothers gathered around to look at him. Finally Mother Duck said, "My baby! You are all grown up. But you're no duck; you're not one of us," she said, "you belong with that flock over there."

Tears streamed down Ugly Duckling's face. To hide the tears, Ugly Duckling bent his neck and saw his whole reflection in the water for the first time! He was large and all white with a black bill. He did look like the white birds in the other flock. He was stunned.

Ugly Duckling swam towards this flock of white birds to get a closer look, even though he was scared that they would hiss or hit or bite him. As he got nearer, the other white birds noticed him and swam towards him. They seemed friendly. They stared at each other. "My lost baby!" shrieked Mama Swan, "I knew there was another egg!" Mama Swan also had one brown and one blue eye.

"If we are not ducks, what are we?" asked Ugly Duckling.

"We are the mighty, beautiful members of the Cygnus Olor swan species, also known as the mute swans. We use our wings to communicate. We are admired everywhere we go," Mama Swan said proudly. "Oh, you're so beautiful, my baby!"

"Welcome home!" the Cygnus Olar mute swans said, flapping their wings with joy as they surrounded Ugly Duckling.

THE TOWN MOUSE AND THE COUNTRY MOUSE

nce upon a time in a bustling town there lived a mouse. Town Mouse considered himself a savvy city slicker who knew his way about town and who could get whatever he needed. He especially enjoyed his home in a large mansion on Main Street, since the Cowbell family often had dinner parties. There were always lots of delicious leftovers such as exotic cheeses, crackers, pies and cakes, always left on the dining room table overnight.

One day, Town Mouse decided to visit his cousin. He hitched a ride on a car bumper to the country, and jumped off when he neared the Country Mouse's home. Country Mouse lived in a small farmer's house.

Country Mouse was thrilled to see his city cousin, and welcomed him heartily. They sat and conversed with each other in sign language. Their eyes were bright and expressive. Their whiskers twittered, sagged, or bristled, depending on what they were talking about. Their faces and bodies were animated. They often laughed at old memories and new stories. Country Mouse went to his pantry and brought out beans, corn, and some stale bread.

"Humph! Is that all that this entire house has to offer?" exclaimed Town Mouse with disdain, turning his nose up at this country offering.

"Yes, but we live well and we are happy," responded Country Mouse.

"Bah! You come with me to the city and you will see what real food is!" Town Mouse retorted. "Then you will wonder how you could ever have lived in the country."

The two mice caught a ride on a farmer's wagon and journeyed to town. They hopped off at Main Street where Town Mouse lived. By then, it was night time and most of the lights in the mansion were turned off. This meant that the residents were sleeping.

"OK, follow me!" Town Mouse said as he clambered into the house through a slightly open window. Country Mouse followed Town Mouse through the window and through the large library and through the tea room into the spacious dining room. As expected, cheeses, jam and cakes were still on the table. He knew that in the morning the maid would come to put these away.

Country Mouse's eyes bulged as he saw the gourmet foods awaiting them. "Whoa, what a feast!" he signed to Town Mouse.

"Stop signing!" Town Mouse signed, using very small signs in a low area of his body. "Signing is not permitted in this house. If you sign, the dogs will start barking!"

But it was too late. The table started vibrating and the mice bounced around. Two dogs were barking and jumping up at the edge of the table to try and capture the signing mice.

"What's happening?" gasped Country Mouse, his heart beating rapidly.

"It's the Dog Sign Police. Fear not, they won't catch us," Town Mouse explained nonchalantly. "They're a nuisance, but it's worth it to dine on this feast, don't you agree?"

The more they signed to each other, the more violently the dogs barked and jumped up and down. Country Mouse could see their teeth gnashing as their heads bobbed over the shaking table. He could almost feel the moist heat of their breath.

"We better run off now before Mr. and Mrs. Cowbell wake up and catch us," said Town Mouse. They jumped up, scurried up the chandelier, and dashed through the electrical opening into the hollows of the ceiling.

Once in the safety of the ceiling, Town Mouse turned around and saw Country Mouse skittering in the other direction. Town Mouse caught up with Country Mouse and tugged at his tail. "Wait! Where are you going?"

"I'm going home. Goodbye, dear cousin," replied Country Mouse, still quivering with fear.

"Why?" asked Town Mouse incredulously. "You just got here!"

"Yes," Country Mouse replied. "I'd rather use my beautiful sign language without fear, and eat beans, corn, and stale bread, than eat fancy foods and be forbidden to use sign language."

MORAL: The freedom to converse in signs without fear is as essential as food, water, and air.

CINDERELLA

nce upon a time in a faraway land called Amina, a couple welcomed their long-awaited child with much joy. They named the baby Terrella, in combined honor of his mother Teresa and her mother Maybella. When Terrella was three months old, they realized she was Deaf. Fortunately, Terrella's father had a Deaf cousin who used Amina Sign Language (ASL). The Deaf cousin was immediately hired to teach the family ASL.

It so happened that Terrella was blessed with beauty and brains. With her parents' devotion and use of ASL, Terrella blossomed. By the time she was one year old, she knew many signs and could form short sentences and recite nursery rhymes. As she grew, she became more and more fluent in both languages, had wonderful self-confidence, and loved to read as well as to play and sign-sing with other children. She loved the old family dog, Theodore, who also adored her. Old Dog Theo learned how to follow commands in signs, such as sit, shake, roll over, and even play dead.

One gloomy day, Terrella's mom became very ill. After a week, she passed away. Terrella was inconsolable.

Her dad hugged Terrella, pointed to the brightest star of the evening and said, "See that brilliant star to the right of the Big Dipper? That's your mother. She will always be there for you." But heartbroken Terrella still moped around the house and wouldn't eat.

Her dad decided Terrella needed a new mother. One day he brought home a new wife who was quite plain-looking. She had two daughters about the same age as Terrella.

"Terrella, see what I brought you? A new mother and two new sisters!" Dad signed to Terrella. "I want to make you happy." His new wife's eyes widened when she saw her husband signing. Terella was Deaf!

The new wife thought, "Deaf?! How pathetic. And she uses sign language. How disgusting! And now she was part of the family. How burdensome!"

Her eyes squinted as she gingerly extended her hand to Terrella, and she mustered a weak smile that revealed gnarly yellow teeth. Her two daughters snickered, but did their best to smile and greet their new stepsister. Their crooked teeth, just like their mother's, showed through their tight smiles. In the meanwhile, their eyes roved around their new home. It was a huge mansion with many large rooms filled with fancy furniture and precious paintings.

Terrella was shocked her dad had remarried so suddenly, but she loved her dad dearly and wanted more than anything to see him happy. So she smiled radiantly, her white teeth gleaming like pearls as her big eyes took in her new family members. She curtsied low to the ground, took the new stepmother's hand, kissed it, and signed, "I'm glad to meet you. Welcome home." She also tried to pet the cat they brought with them, but quickly withdrew her hand when FatCat tried to claw it.

Stepmother exclaimed to Dad, "What'd she say? Doesn't she speak?"

Dad replied, "ASL is her natural language and she's fluent in English, too. You'll learn ASL quickly."

"Sure," Stepmother muttered under her breath. "Over my dead body. She must learn to speak first."

Weeks passed and neither Stepmother nor Stepsisters made any effort to learn ASL or to reach out to Terrella. Stepmother constantly complained about the amount of work she had to do—supervising the servants who did the cooking and cleaning —and she didn't have time for that ASL nonsense.

Dad gradually realized he had made a mistake in marrying this woman. He grieved deeply, and became withdrawn, much to Terrella's dismay. One day the family discovered Dad slumped in his armchair in the library. The doctor said Dad had died from a broken heart. A glimmer of a sly grin crept over Stepmother's face, one that she did not try to suppress.

After the funeral, Stepmother spoke to Terrella, "Your father is dead, and I've inherited everything. You will do exactly as I tell you to do if you wish to stay here. We will save money by letting the servants go. You will do their work."

Terrella, not understanding Stepmother's spoken words, asked, "What?"

Stepmother grabbed Terrella's arm and dragged her to the kitchen. "Look here, little girl! You cook, you clean everything, and you keep the fireplace going," she gestured to the bewildered girl. "You sleep in the attic from now on. Start now. Don't bother me." She abruptly turned and left the room.

Terrella's eyes widened in amazement at Stepmother's rapid change in attitude, looked down, and saw FatCat smirking. Old Dog Theo snarled at FatCat before slinking under the table, tail between his legs.

The stepsisters giggled with delight and started bossing poor Terrella around. "She's nothing more than a dumb mute animal," they exclaimed. They went into her bedroom and took all of Terrella's frocks and necklaces for themselves, squealing with glee. However, for some reason unfathomable to them, they didn't look as good in Terrella's clothes as she did. They immediately were jealous of Terrella and the injustice of her beauty.

Cleaning out the cinders in the fireplace daily, Terrella soon became dirty with soot. Her stepsisters laughed in delight, and screamed, "Look at her! Covered with cinder! Let's call her Cinderella from now on!" Cinderella, relegated to her new role and her new name, gamely adjusted and decided to make the best of it until she could figure out what to do. The days passed, and Cinderella sign-sung as she worked.

> CLEAN, CLEAN ALL-DAY,
> QUIETLY, QUIETLY.
> COOK, COOK ALL-DAY,
> QUIETLY, QUIETLY.
> SWEEP, SWEEP ALL-DAY,
> QUIETLY, QUIETLY.
> FUTURE, FUTURE, NEW!
> QUIET, QUIET, NO-MORE!

In the kitchen, Cinderella noticed mice. She was lonely, and craved company. She decided to befriend the mice and fed them corn kernels. Bluebirds chirped on the window ledge for their share of the corn kernels. Cinderella sign-sung as she worked, and the animals swayed in beat with her signs. One of Cinderella's favorite sign-songs was her dream of escaping her servitude, and taking her animal friends with her.

> PATIENCE, PATIENCE, WORK-WORK-WORK
> OUTSIDE, OUTSIDE, SUNNY- SUNNY-SUNNY
> SOON, SOON, ESCAPE-ESCAPE-ESCAPE
> WILL, WILL, FINISH-FINISH-FINISH
> TOGETHER, TOGETHER, FREE-FREE-FREE.
> PATIENCE, PATIENCE, CONTINUE-CONTINUE-
> CONTINUE.
> DREAM, DREAM, MUST-MUST-MUST!

At night, from her attic window, Cinderella's gaze would always turn to the brightest star of the night, where her dad said her mom was. Whenever she saw the star, she knew everything would work out in the end.

Days became weeks and weeks became months. One day the mailman brought a special engraved envelope addressed to "The Fair Maidens of Amina." At dinner time, Cinderella presented the envelope to Stepmother, who opened it and smiled as she read the contents to her two daughters. Cinderella peered over Stepmother's shoulder to read the card.

"All the fair maidens of the kingdom of Amina are cordially invited to the Royal Ball at the Castle to meet the Prince," the card said. The Prince was seeking a wife and the ball would take place in three days.

Stepsisters squealed with delight. "Ooooh! Prince wants to marry. Me, me, me!" both exclaimed at the same time. They looked at each other in surprise, and began bickering.

Stepmother said, "Shhh. One of you must marry the prince. We don't have enough money left to pay taxes on this house or to buy daily necessities."

Cinderella smiled and said, "I'll go to the ball, too."

"You? You don't have a dress!" Stepsisters answered.

"I'll borrow one," Cinderella said.

"Oh no, you can't," Stepsisters snorted.

Stepmother then dragged Cinderella to the attic and locked her up. "No, no, you can't do this to me," Cinderella pleaded as she pounded on the door. But the door wouldn't budge. Through the keyhole, Cinderella watched as Stepmother descended the spiral stairway, a great sneer on her face. Cinderella fell on her bed of hay and sobbed and sobbed. The invitation was for all maidens, including her. It just wasn't fair. She continued to sob until she became so tired that she stopped.

When Cinderella finally looked up, she saw her friends the mice and the birds sadly watching her. Tears were also rolling down their faces.

"What'll we do?" asked Cinderella, tears still on her face.

Mouse Leader responded with a determined look:

> GIVE-UP, NO!
> WITH DREAM
> WITH LOVE
> CAN CHANGE

IMPOSSIBLE → POSSIBLE
WITH DREAM
WITH LOVE
IMPOSSIBLE → POSSIBLE!

Cinderella felt much better and not so alone.

Together, they developed a game plan.

The sky-blue velveteen curtains in Cinderella's attic room would be cut up and sewn into a gown. The birds would fly through an open window into the sewing room one floor below for a needle, thread, and buttons. The mice would sneak into Cinderella's old bedroom to get her mother's pearl necklace from its secret hiding place. The Mouse Leader would recover the bedroom key somehow from Stepmother so Cinderella could leave her room and ride to the ball with Stepmother and Stepsisters.

They chanted as they worked:

GIVE-UP, NO!
WITH DREAM
WITH LOVE
CAN CHANGE
IMPOSSIBLE → POSSIBLE
WITH DREAM
WITH LOVE
IMPOSSIBLE → POSSIBLE!

The mice and birds helped Cinderella cut up the velveteen drapes, piece together the dress, and stitch it together. They added pearl buttons along the back of the dress. They used the lace curtains as a sash for the dress. They found a brooch under a dresser and pinned it to the dress. With her mom's pearl necklace, Cinderella looked drop-dead stunning. But she was still locked in her room. She looked out the window. In a few minutes, Stepmother and Stepsisters would get in their horse-drawn coach for the ball.

In the meantime, Mouse Leader was struggling to reach the hook on the kitchen wall where the key to Cinderella's room hung. FatCat sat directly under the hook, a giant leer plastered on his face. Old Dog Theo sized up the situation, mustered up his strength, and started snarling at FatCat, frightening him away. Mouse Leader quickly climbed up onto Old Dog Theo's head and snatched the key from the wall hook, and away they ran up the winding stairs all the way to the attic. They fumbled with getting the key into the keyhole until finally it clicked and the door swung open, much to their relief.

Cinderella gathered up the hem of her dress and flew down the stairway to the front door just in time to join Stepmother and Stepsisters as they were boarding the coach.

Stepmother and Stepsisters looked at Cinderella in dumbfounded amazement. It was not only that she had escaped, but also that she looked absolutely stunning. A dark cloud of jealously came over their faces.

"Hey, that's my brooch, you stole it!" Stepsister screamed as she tore it off the dress, ripping the dress.

"That's my pearl necklace," the other Stepsister shrieked as she yanked it off, breaking the thread and sending the pearls in all directions.

"And my lace!" said Stepmother as the Stepsisters ripped the sash into pieces. A look of satisfaction came over their faces as they boarded the coach and took off, leaving Cinderella in the dust. Cinderella now was ragged and devastated.

The mice, bluebirds and Old Dog Theo sadly gathered around Cinderella, saying, "Don't cry, something will work out."

Cinderella shook her head and said, "It's no use. I'll run away as soon as I can." The mice started picking up the pearls and putting them in a knapsack. Cinderella looked up at the stars, threw up her arms, and exclaimed, "What heinous crime have I done that I should be so punished like this?!"

Suddenly, the brightest star of the evening blazed in response, and grew bigger and bigger. Cinderella and her friends stared at it in astonishment as it drew nearer and nearer to them, landing in front of them. They rubbed their eyes as the blaze faded, revealing a portly woman robed in white. She had a genuine smile and her eyes twinkled as she looked at Cinderella.

"Dear Cinderella, I'm your fairy godmother," she signed gently, "Why are you crying?"

"Because I can't go to the ball."

"Nonsense, my dear child, of course you can."

"But how? My dress is shredded." Cinderella pointed to her clothes.

"Oh, that? Pshaw, that's nothing! Stand up and get ready to go. Now, all together with me, let's sign-sing the magic spell."

"What magic spell?"

"This one!"

> GIVE-UP, NO!
> WITH DREAM
> WITH LOVE
> CAN CHANGE
> IMPOSSIBLE → POSSIBLE
> WITH DREAM
> WITH LOVE
> IMPOSSIBLE → POSSIBLE!

As they chanted, a swirl of dazzling fairy stars enveloped the group. As the stars settled, Cinderella was astounded to see her dress transformed into a magnificent gown, laced with exquisite rose-shaped ribbons with pearl centers. Her mom's pearl necklace was restored and back around her neck! On her feet were sparkling glass slippers. But her animal friends were gone.

"No, not gone," Fairy Godmother reassured the worried Cinderella, as she worked her magic further to transform the mice into fine horses, Old Dog Theo into a footman, and Mouse Leader into the coach driver. A pumpkin was instantly transformed into a golden coach. FatCat peered from behind a bush to see what was happening and Godmother instantly turned him into a stone statue. The group erupted into joyous laughter.

"Now, my child, there's no time to waste. You need to leave now for the ball. However, when the clock strikes midnight, the spell will be broken and everything will revert back. Now, go and have a great time!" With that, Fairy Godmother started dissolving into a swirling blaze of light.

"Thank you, thank you, Mom, and Fairy Godmother," said Cinderella as she watched the light whoosh back into the night sky. The golden coach sped away and soon arrived at the palace.

In the grand ballroom, Cinderella caught a glimpse of the prince. He was tall and handsome. His father, the king, had set up this ball as his last attempt to marry off his son. The king looked happy because the prince had promised he'd choose a wife tonight. Yet the prince did not look comfortable as he looked over the ladies to decide which one he would invite to dance with him. He spotted Cinderella in the back of the room, behind the crowd, and was captivated by her beauty.

"Yes, she might be the one," Prince thought.

The crowd parted as Prince made his way to the back. Everyone turned her head to see which fair maiden the prince was choosing. Stepsisters screeched, "Who's that? Why, it's Cinderella! No, it can't be!"

Indeed, it was Cinderella, the loveliest maiden in the land and absolutely dazzling! Before Stepsisters could do anything, Prince gently took Cinderella's hand and led her to the dance floor. Gasps, oohs, and ahhs filled the ballroom, overpowering Stepsisters' hissing.

Cinderella was shocked and didn't know what to think. It was a dream come true even if it couldn't be real. She looked up at Prince and smiled. Her smile was dazzling, making Prince's heart thump so loudly Cinderella could dance to the beat of it.

Cinderella's heart was also pounding as she pondered, "What will happen when he finds out I'm Deaf?!"

The other lords and knights asked the rest of the maidens to dance. King beamed seeing Prince on the dance floor with such a beauty. "He'll finally settle down and continue the family dynasty," King thought.

Prince whispered into Cinderella's ear as they danced, "What's your name and where have you been all my life?" Sensing Prince was talking, Cinderella looked into Prince's intense eyes and tried to figure what to do. This was a dream come true, but it'd be shattered the minute Prince discovered she was Deaf. There were many other maidens in the room; he'd go and pick someone else. What should she do?

Cinderella looked at Prince and smiled broadly. "It's now or never. Let the truth ring true," she thought to herself, as she started to sign, "Thank you for picking me to dance with you. You made my dream come true, even if only briefly. Thank you." Cinderella let go of Prince, curtsied and made her way through the crowd to the back of the room. Inside, she was shaking as she thought, "He did not understand what I said anyway and I'm sure he's glad I left." She bit her lip. "If only..." At least she had this memory to sustain her until her next stage in life.

Suddenly she felt someone tapping on her shoulder from behind, stopping her. She swung around and looked. It was Prince!

He looked at her and signed, "Why are you leaving? Please stay."

Cinderella could hardly believe her eyes, "You know sign language?! How?"

Prince responded, "Sign language is important to know. When we are at war, we can sign battle plans to each other from a distance. Or when we are taken prisoner, we can communicate secretly to each other. Or we can communicate quietly as we overtake our enemies at night. Sign language is cherished in our army. I'm thrilled you know it, too!"

Cinderella rubbed her eyes in astonishment. "Is this still a dream?!"

Before she could say anything, Prince put his arm around her and signed, "Let's continue dancing!"

And dance they did, around and around the room. As they danced, they chatted. Hours flew by. They had eyes only for each other. They seemed perfectly made for each other. Cinderella looked around the room and when she saw the look of disgust on Stepsisters and Stepmother's faces, she tried to suppress a smile. Above their heads hung a grandfather clock, and she saw that it would soon strike midnight! At midnight, the spell would be broken. She'd turn back to looking like a raggedy servant. She couldn't bear to have Prince see her like that! She had to break away and get back home now.

As Prince was about to kiss Cinderella, she broke away and dashed down the royal stairway, losing a glass slipper on the way. The golden coach and the driver, footman, and horses were anxiously awaiting her. She leapt into her golden coach and it sped down the road. The spell ended two minutes later, near Cinderella's home.

Cinderella, in her ragged dress, was surrounded by her animal friends and pieces of a broken pumpkin. Was it only a dream? Her other glass slipper was still on her foot! Maybe it wasn't a dream, after all.

Cinderella lifted her eyes to the sky and signed, "Thank you again, Mom and Fairy Godmother. It was the best night of my life." She walked back home and up the spiral stairway back to her room in the attic. Through her bedroom window, she looked up again. The star right of the Big Dipper winked and twinkled brightly at her.

The next morning, Cinderella served breakfast to Stepmother and Stepsisters. They seemed to be nice and tried to gesture to Cinderella for the first time. "Please teach us ASL," they implored.

"Why now?" a puzzled Cinderella wondered.

As Cinderella cleared away the dishes, she saw the Daily Drum newspaper on the kitchen table. A headline read, "ASL Maiden Flees Ball." The line below read, "Hunt for Signing Bride Begins." The king's trusted men would visit all homes in the kingdom to search for the signing bride.

"Aha! That's why they want to sign—they want to be the Signing Bride," Cinderella thought. Her heart began to race as she realized Prince was looking for her, and she thought, "But I look like a mess!"

Soon, the doorbell rang, and the animals scurried around, showing Cinderella that someone was at the door. Stepmother stepped across the kitchen door threshold and snarled, "You stay here in the kitchen. That's an order." She slammed the door behind her and bolted it.

Through openings between the door panels, Cinderella watched both Stepsisters struggle to put on the glass slipper, but in vain. The King's soldier signed to the sisters, "It doesn't fit; it can't be yours." They responded with made-up signs, only to get looks of disgust from the soldiers, who all were fluent in sign language. The fake signs confirmed that neither Stepsister was the ASL maiden.

As the soldiers started to leave the house, Cinderella banged on the kitchen door loudly, and the soldiers looked back. "What's that?" inquired the soldiers.

"It's nobody, only a lowly chambermaid," Stepmother replied.

Pushing Stepmother aside, the soldiers said, "We have our orders to have every maiden try on the shoe," and flung open the door. They saw Cinderella, and approached her. They asked her to try on the slipper.

Stepmother, in an attempt to thwart the soldiers, struck the crystal shoe and sent it crashing to the floor, where it broke into hundreds of pieces.

Cinderella promptly brought out the other crystal slipper, glistening in the light, from her apron pocket, identical to the one that had just broken. Stepmother furiously grabbed it out of Cinderella's hand and it, too, broke into pieces.

Dismay hung over the room.

The soldiers had a Plan B, as all good soldiers should. They quizzed Cinderella in sign language without using their voices, "Where did you get the other slipper?"

"It's mine," Cinderella signed back, "I wore it to the ball last night. One slipper came off when I ran away from the ball."

"Hallelujah, she's fluent in ASL. She had the other slipper. She's the one!" the soldiers sign-shouted together in glee. They escorted Cinderella outside into the king's coach, and sped away to the palace.

Prince and Cinderella got married, and lived happily together in the palace. Schools everywhere in the kingdom started to teach sign language along with English and other languages. Amina became known as the land of equality, justice and full access for all its people. Everyone lived happily ever after, including Stepmother and Stepsisters who continued to dwell in Cinderella's father's house, with annual taxes and fees waived by Prince and Cinderella, on the condition they learned ASL.

> Love trumps hate.
> When true love is your fate,
> It's worth the wait,
> For love always trumps hate.

SNOW WHITE

n a faraway place, there lived a most beautiful queen. Queen prided herself on her looks, and had a Magic Mirror that could answer any question Queen asked. Queen looked at her image daily in the mirror, admiring her beauty.

Daily, Queen asked the Magic Mirror, "Who is the fairest lady in the land?"

Daily, Magic Mirror responded, "You are, my queen."

Queen had married King shortly after her sister, the original queen, died in childbirth. The baby girl had raven-black hair, a fair complexion, and rosy-pink lips. They named the beautiful baby Snow White.

King and Queen discovered that Snow White was Deaf. They were shocked because she did not look or act Deaf. She was alert to her surroundings. Since she did not speak, she seemed to compensate for it by trying to gesture. King and Queen were at a loss about what to do. They called in the Royal Palace doctor to see what could be done. The doctor informed them that Snow White could indeed be taught how to listen and speak. It would be a challenge, but it could be done. A call went out from the Royal Palace for a top-notch speech teacher. After interviewing a few candidates, they decided to hire Mr. Braidswart, whose credentials were impressive. He had a reputation for successfully teaching deaf-mutes to listen and speak.

Mr. Braidswart moved into the Royal Palace and started lessons immediately with Snow White. Snow White did not like this big man with the beady eyes whose lips moved incessantly.

Sometimes his mustache covered his lips. Sometimes he had bad breath. Sometimes he inadvertently spat on her when he was teaching her a sound. Sometimes he gagged her when making her practice her Ks and Gs. He made her sit on her hands and repeat words over and over again. She felt like a caged parrot.

"Queen Mother," Snow White pleaded, "please stop my lessons with Mr. Braidswart. I want to read and write. I want to learn more about everything. I don't want to waste so much time on speech and listening. I want to play. I don't have friends other than a few children of the servants."

However, Queen ignored Snow White's pleas. "My dear child, you must hear and speak to survive in this hearing world, especially as a member of the royal family. The doctor said you can learn to hear and speak if you would only try harder. You must practice more!"

As months turned into years, Snow White blossomed into a lovely maiden. Her fair complexion and eyes were exquisitely framed by her raven-black hair. Heads turned wherever Snow White went. But she was not happy. Even with intensive speech and listening instruction, she struggled to make herself understood or to understand other people. She was forbidden to use her hands to gesture because it was deemed unbecoming. Often she would ask what people such as her parents were talking about during dinner, and was always told, "Shhh. We will explain later." But the explanations were always brief. She was frustrated but did not know what she could do. She took refuge in her books, which opened the doors to the world for her.

As Snow White grew up, she often saw Queen looking at her with a stern expression. "Why does she always seem mad at me? What did I do wrong?" Snow White wondered to herself.

Unknown to Snow White, Queen continued her daily ritual of looking into her Magic Mirror and asking, "Who is the fairest lady in the land?"

And daily as always, Magic Mirror responded, "You are, my queen."

One day, when Snow White turned 16, as Queen feared, Magic Mirror responded, "You are, my Queen, but very soon Snow White will surpass you in beauty."

Queen was livid. She turned white and then purple with rage. "This cannot be allowed to happen. I must be the fairest one in the land. I will not be outdone by a deaf-mute! Snow White must go!"

Queen hatched a plan. One day, when, Queen accompanied King on a trip, she would have one of her trusted soldiers secretly take Snow White deep into the woods and kill her.

And so Snow White found herself deep in the woods on horseback with a soldier. She did not understand what was happening. It seemed to be a nice ride, and the woods were cool. After an hour or two, they stopped abruptly in the middle of nowhere, and got off the horse. The soldier said "I cannot bear to kill you. Please run away, as fast as you can, as far away as you can."

Not comprehending, Snow White said "What?" but the soldier shooed her away, mounted his horse, turned around, and galloped away. The soldier, on his way back to the palace, stabbed a fox and removed its heart, as evidence for Queen that he had complied with her order.

The nice, deep woods transformed to a dark, cold, foreboding place as the sun set. Snow White's heart pounded, but she kept her head. She had to keep going and find shelter for the night. She started walking and running, and some of the branches hit at her as she passed by. After what seemed like hours, she saw a clearing in the woods, revealing a small house. She'd go there to ask for help.

Snow White knocked at the door. There was no response, although the lights were on. She could see people inside. She knocked louder but there was still no response. She saw a button next to the door, and pressed it. The lights in the house flashed, frightening Snow White. "Maybe it is a haunted house?" she thought to herself.

The door flung open. Seven dwarfs peered up at Snow White.

"Who are you? Where from? What's your name?" they signed.

Snow White was taken aback by their gesticulating hands.

"I'm Snow White," she stammered, "I need a place to stay tonight."

The dwarfs could lipread a bit and they excitedly interpreted Snow White's spoken words into signs for each other. "That's Snow White! We know about her. She is beautiful!" They were immediately love-struck.

Snow White said, "I'm sorry, I don't know how to talk with my hands. Is it hard to learn?"

The dwarfs giggled and fell all over each other assuring Snow White that she could learn and it would be easy.

"Are you Deaf like me?" inquired Snow White.

"Yes, yes!" they responded with big grins. "Same as you!"

It was the first time Snow White met other Deaf people. And they seemed comfortable signing. But her teacher had said signing was bad. She was confused, and gestured, "May I stay here tonight?"

"Yes, yes! Are you hungry? We have stew," the friendliest dwarf gestured. The others nodded excitedly, running around to get dinner ready.

As she ate, the dwarfs introduced themselves as Axelrod, Clerc, Davila, Foster, Schreiber, Valli, and Veditz. In the room were seven beds, each wooden headboard with its occupant's initials engraved on it: CA, LC, RD, AF, FS, CV and GV.

The dwarfs put two sofas together and gestured for Snow White to sleep there. As Snow White lay there, her anxieties started to fade away as she felt safe, and she dozed off.

The next morning, the dwarfs bustled about, making breakfast. Snow White woke up, rubbed her eyes, and remembered where she was. The dwarfs explained that they had to go to work, but that Clerc would stay home with Snow White and teach her sign language as well as show her around. Clerc was an extraordinary teacher, and Snow White picked up on signs quickly.

That evening, she helped prepare dinner for the dwarfs. They sat around the dinner table, chatting in sign language as they ate. Snow White was surprised to see how much she could understand although her attempts to sign were still developing. For the first time, she felt included.

A daily routine developed. Snow White took care of the home and the garden, and prepared dinner while all the dwarfs went to work. But the dwarfs admonished her daily, "Snow White, please stay home. Lock the gate outside and lock the house door. Do not answer the door if a stranger comes."

"Why?" Snow White asked.

"Because Queen hates you and if she knows you are here, she will come and get you."

"How do you know that?"

"The Deaf grapevine is the best source of news. Deaf people take care of each other. We know about you and what happened," they explained.

More days, and then weeks, passed. Snow White busied herself around the home, read books, made jam and quilts, and cooked delicious dinners. Her favorite time of the day was dinnertime. She could understand the discussions and as her confidence grew, she participated more. She loved the conversations, which were sometimes serious, sometimes funny.

Often the dwarfs shared stories and experiences, such as the time when a Deaf person went into a cafe and sat down on a stool next to a stranger. The stranger tried to strike up a conversation, and the Deaf person got out a pen and paper. They started writing back and forth. Another stranger sat on the other side of the Deaf person and soon he too joined in the conversation by reading notes and writing back and forth. The Deaf person had to leave the cafe. He bid his new companions farewell, and as he was leaving, he looked back at them and chuckled as he saw them still writing notes to each other!

Sometimes the dwarfs discussed politics, human rights, and quality access. They worked at the National Office of Deaf People. They advocated for Deaf people's rights to get jobs, to own land, to marry, and to have children. They supported sign language for all babies. Snow White felt overwhelmed at first; it was so different from her family's beliefs, yet it felt so right to her. She had finally found her Deaf center. She participated in discussions more and more. She could not understand why sign language was forbidden in the Palace and promised herself that she would make a difference in the lives of families with Deaf babies.

When Queen returned to the Palace after her trip, she made a beeline for Magic Mirror.

Queen asked Magic Mirror, "Who is the fairest lady in the land?"

Magic Mirror responded, "Snow White is, my Queen."

"What?!?" sputtered Queen. "But Snow White is dead."

"Not dead. Just Deaf."

"Is she alive? Where?" demanded Queen.

Magic Mirror revealed an image showing Snow White happily living in the house of the seven dwarfs, on the other side of the forest.

"No! I will not allow it," shrieked Queen.

Queen devised a plan to kill Snow White, and she would do it personally. But she had to change herself into an ugly withered hag, with a hideous nose covered in warts.

"There. Snow White will not recognize me now," Queen said with satisfaction. "Now I'll poison half of an apple and give it to her."

Queen set out on horseback for the seven dwarfs' house. She had a basket of beautiful red apples, half of each one poisoned. Finally she arrived at the cottage, and rang the doorbell. The lights flashed and Snow White looked through the window to see who it was. There stood a shriveled old lady, selling apples. Snow White motioned that she was not interested, and waved her away.

But the old lady persisted, ringing the doorbell again and again until Snow White opened the door just a crack. She kept the door chain on it.

"Here, pick a delicious apple," the old lady said.

"No, thank you," Snow White gestured as she shook her head.

"Oh, but you must. See, I'll take a bite first." The old lady carefully took a bite out of an apple, and then turned it around to the poisoned side and offered Snow White a taste, through the chained door.

"Oh, all right." Snow White took a bite, hoping that the old lady would leave after that. But Snow White immediately felt dizzy, and fainted.

The old lady chuckled, "Heee, heee, heee!" and rode away in delight.

When the dwarfs arrived home from work, they were shocked to see Snow White crumpled on the floor. Rushing into the house through the back door, they saw an apple in her hand. Veditz checked Snow White's mouth and found the apple peel still in it. He removed it and tried to revive her, but could not wake her.

He looked mournfully at the other dwarfs and said that Snow White had been poisoned, but because she had not swallowed the apple peel, she would not die. She would only go into a deep and permanent slumber from which she might never awaken. "Oh no, oh no," cried the dwarfs.

The dwarfs made a beautiful casket. The top was made out of glass, so the dwarfs could keep an eye on her. If Snow White came to, she could see where she was. They placed Snow White in the casket and put it in the forest, near their daily path to work. They planted poppies and lupines around the casket. They visited the casket every day, always sad but hopeful. Days and days passed. Snow White looked so beautiful, and the dwarfs never lost hope.

One day, as the dwarfs were walking back home from work, they spied a man on horseback near the casket. Hiding themselves as they watched, they saw that it was Prince from the next kingdom.

Prince dismounted his horse to get a better look at the fair maiden in the casket. She looked so beautiful and so life-like that Prince decided to open the casket and examine her closely. She looked even more beautiful and Prince immediately fell in love with her. He bent over, lifted her slightly and kissed her on her ruby-red lips.

Snow White's eyes fluttered.

Prince's heart fluttered.

Her hands then fluttered, "Who are you? What's happening?"

"What?" said Prince, not understanding sign language.

"You don't know sign language?" Snow White responded. A look of disappointment crossed her face as she lay back down in the casket. "Goodbye!" she said, closing the glass top and resuming her deep slumber.

Prince stood up from his kneeling position, his head spinning with puzzlement. "What did I do wrong?" he asked himself.

Just then, the seven dwarfs approached him. They wrote notes to Prince, explaining that Snow White loved being Deaf and using sign language. Upon being liberated and finding her Deaf identity, Snow White did not want to go back to her old way of life.

Prince looked in astonishment at the dwarfs. He bowed and motioned, "Thank you," before mounting his steed. As he rode away, he vowed, "I shall learn sign language and I shall return!"

THE LION AND THE MOUSE

 ing Lion was napping peacefully in the jungle, when suddenly he sensed something climbing over him. He woke up and saw a little mouse running up and down his body. Lion was incensed at having his nap interrupted. He placed his huge paw on Mouse and decided to make a snack out of the little critter. As he drew Mouse to his mouth, Mouse waved his paws and signed, "Oh, King, please forgive me! I did not know that you were napping. Please free me. Someday I will do you a favor, too."

Lion, who did not know sign language, did not understand Mouse. But he was fascinated with Mouse's moving hands. He put his paw down so he could see Mouse better. Mouse knew Lion did not understand sign language, so he pantomimed that if Lion let him go, he would help Lion some day.

"How can a little mouse like you help me?! Especially a Deaf mouse like you!?" Lion guffawed. He thought the idea so funny that he released his hold and set Mouse free.

A few days later, Lion fell into a trap. Hunters came and prodded Lion from the trap into a steel cage. Lion roared and chewed at the bars to no avail. Worn out, he flopped down on the cage floor and wondered what would become of him. Nighttime fell.

In the moonlight, Lion suddenly spotted Mouse. One of the hunters was with Mouse. Lion saw Mouse signing to the hunter that Lion was his friend and to unlock the cage door. The hunter signed that he would.

Mouse hopped on the Lion's mane as the cage opened. In the darkness of the night, Lion slunk out of the cage and raced away, far away to a safe place, as Mouse hung onto his mane. Lion looked at Mouse and asked, "How did you do that?"

Mouse gestured, "I looked at the hunters and recognized that one was Deaf, like me. I could tell by the look in his eyes. I began signing to him, and explained that you were my friend. He agreed to let you go."

MORAL: Compassion may create great friendships.

THE THREE LITTLE PIGS

 ay yonder on a faraway farm unknown to many, there lived three Deaf Pigs. When they graduated from school, their mother told them it was time for them to go out in the world, seek their fortune, and build their own homes. Bidding their parents a teary farewell, they packed up their few belongings and their lunches in knapsacks and set out on their journey on their short little legs.

Fifteen minutes later, they went around the first bend in the road and could no longer see their home.

Pig1 exclaimed, "This is it! Let's settle here. There are nearby farms where we can work."

Pig2 tilted his head, lowered his eyebrows, and squinted and remarked, "It's too close to home and I don't want to become a farmhand. It's too hard."

Pig3 agreed, adding that they might become the farmer's dinner should there be any disagreements.

So the three pigs kept trudging along the winding road. Three hours later, they came upon a grassy clearing surrounded by a beautiful citrus grove. They sat down to retrieve their sandwiches from their knapsacks. As they were eating, Pig2 said, "What a beautiful spot. Let's settle here."

Pig1 said, "Fine. I'm tired of walking. We can begin to build our home now and have a roof over our heads by nightfall."

Pig3 said sternly, "No, no. This is in the middle of nowhere. Where will we find jobs, let alone materials to build our home?"

"Awwww," sighed Pig1 and Pig2 in almost perfect harmony. "We are tired and the fruits around here will keep our tummies satiated. No need to work."

"No, no," Pig3 responded emphatically, "pigs cannot live on fruit alone. We need to live near a village where we can get jobs as bakers or shopkeepers or tailors. Besides, Deaf pigs need to live near a community of others like ourselves so we can have friends, a social life, and ways to keep up with news."

Expecting further resistance from Pig1 and Pig2, Pig3 continued, "Besides, we can meet cute Deaf pigs in the village!"

With that, all three pigs nodded in agreement, leaped up and marched down the road with renewed enthusiasm, signing-singing:

> ONWARD-ONWARD, THERE-THERE-THERE,
> HOME-HOME, NEW-NEW-NEW,
> FRIENDS-FRIENDS, MEET-MEET-MEET,
> ONWARD-ONWARD, HOME-HOME-HOME!

As they signed, their heads swayed back and forth, following the rhythm of their signs.

Three hours later, tired and dusty, they finally came upon an open meadow bordered by a forest, and through the meadow ran a sparkling creek. They squealed in delight. They rushed to the creek, splashing their faces and drinking the cool refreshing water.

They spied a "For Sale" sign by the road on the edge of that meadow. There was also a signpost in the shape of an arrow staked next to the sign, "Village, 1/2 mile."

"Here!?" yelped Pig1, turning to look at Pig2.

"Here?!" pleaded Pig2, looking at Pig3.

"Perfect!" stated Pig3, turning to Pig1 and Pig2 and extending his hooves. "Welcome home!"

"PAH! Fine," sighed Pig1 and Pig2, looking around a bit quizzically at the vast wilderness, too tired and too hungry to discuss this further.

"What do we do now?" asked Pig1 and Pig2.

"Let's make camp, warm up the mush, and hit the sack," replied Pig3. "Tomorrow morning we will go to the village to buy this property."

"Buy?!" Pig1 and Pig2 asked incredulously. "With what? We don't have money."

"Well, remember," replied Pig3, "when we were growing up, sometimes we got quarters from relatives. Instead of buying candy like you, I saved my money in my little Dutch Boy bank. Early mornings, when you were sleeping, I delivered newspapers. Into that little Dutch Boy bank the newspaper tips went. When you were out playing and partying, I did my homework, made good grades, and Dad rewarded me. Again the reward money went into my little Dutch Boy bank. So now I hope I have enough for a down payment on the land. We all will need to get jobs to pay off the rest of the loan. Agree?"

"Yes, whatever," replied Pig1 and Pig2 wearily and warily.

They set up a tent and settled in for the night by the campfire. In the pitch black darkness, stars blazed above, but the woods remained dark and foreboding. Suddenly glowering eyes seemed to move around in the woods.

Pig1 and Pig2 shuddered, "Scary! Let's forget all this and go home!"

"Oh, pooh, pooh!" said Pig 3, waving his hooves at Pig1 and Pig2. "These are our neighbors, the fireflies! Also maybe a curious bunny or deer. Harmless!"

The next morning the three pigs trotted off to the village real estate office to learn the cost and terms of buying the property. The office was on Main Street, conveniently located between the bank and the furniture store. The real estate agent, a hefty bull with long, sharp horns, was sitting at his desk, hunched over his papers and scrutinizing them with his spectacles. The three pigs, unsure of how to get his attention without startling him, tiptoed to his desk and waved their hooves in the space between his eyes and the papers.

Startled nonetheless, Bull's head jerked up, his long, menacing horns pointing directly at them scant inches away from their snouts. He bellowed, "What's wrong with you?! Can't you ring the bell instead of trying to give me a heart attack?!"

The three pigs, taken aback by Bull's fierce expression and not understanding what Bull said, pointed to their ears and shook their heads. "You Deaf? Go away. You don't have money or knowledge to buy anything," snarled Bull, motioning with his hoof that they should get lost.

Pig1 and Pig2 turned around to leave but Pig3's blood started to boil. He grabbed a piece of paper and pen and wrote "We want to buy the land up the road from the village. How much will it cost?"

Bull's face broke into a distorted grin. "Hah! How will you pay for it?"

Upon finding that sales price was reasonable, Pig3 wrote that he had more than half of the sale price saved up for the down payment and that they all would get jobs to pay off the rest of the loan within a few years.

Bull's face, now frozen in a sneer, wrote back, "Jobs? You can't hear or talk; what can you do?"

"Deaf pigs can do anything," retorted Pig3. "Pig1 bakes the best cakes and breads and if he can't get a job, he will open his own bakery. Pig2 can fix anything, so he can work at the hardware store or garage and if he can't get a job, he will open his own shop.

I can teach or tutor any subject and if I can't get a job, I will start my own program. Just give us a chance."

With that, Bull's sneer morphed into a gaping mouth. "Okay, here are the papers. Sign here. The bank is next door and the law office is across the street. Good luck. Remember that if you don't pay on time, the town jail is next to the law office. And you'll lose the land and your down payment." Bull's expression of surprise had quickly reverted back to a sneer.

After all the details were taken care of, and with proof of purchase in hoof, the three pigs ambled to the town cafe to celebrate. There they met another Deaf pig, who mentioned that the Village Deaf Club was nearby and signing animals convened there twice weekly.

The three pigs were welcomed enthusiastically into the Deaf Club. They shared that they were moving to the village, and told of their terrifying encounter with Bull. Their new friends advised them to ring the bell next time.

"Bell? What bell?" asked Pigs in unison.

"Doorbell, that's how hearing animals know if someone wants to enter the shop, so they aren't startled," replied the new friends.

Other advice and Deaf-centric solutions for getting around and getting along in town were shared by the old-timers.

The three pigs were ready to build their home. Pig1 wanted something easy and quick. "Let's gather those long stalks of grass in our meadow and build our home. Then we can go and play with our new friends," he said.

Pig2 and Pig3 shook their heads no. Pig2 said, "That isn't sturdy enough and wouldn't last over time." He suggested building a house with twigs and sticks that had fallen on the forest floor.

Pig3 disagreed, "That's not strong enough, either. The house must be able to withstand all elements, rain, hail, and high winds, and who knows what else?"

"No, no, too much work, it's not worth it!" responded Pig1 and Pig2.

The three pigs continued to argue all through the night. They sat around their campfire so they could see each other's signs. Again the stars overhead twinkled brilliantly and glimmers of light floated eerily around the dark woods. The pigs felt like they were being observed, and their hearts were beating as they crawled into their tent for the night.

The three pigs argued all day the next day about how to build their new home. They couldn't come to an agreement. Finally Pig1 said, "I'll just go and build my home with hay. You two do what you want."

Pig2 looked at Pig3 and said, "I still prefer sticks so I'll go ahead with my house."

Pig3 said "Fine, I'll do mine in brick."

Each of the three pigs got to work. Pig1 completed his home in one day, and started laughing at Pig2 and Pig3, still laboring at their houses. By noon the next day, Pig2 completed his home and joined Pig1 at the club, partying with their new friends.

Pig3 continued to build his home, brick by brick, steadily and surely. On the sixth day Pig3's home was finally completed. It was a fine-looking house with glass windows, sturdy doors, and a fireplace for cooking.

Nighttime fell, and the three pigs chatted around the campfire for a little while, celebrating their new homes with s'mores and stories. Again glowing orbs floated around in the woods. Their skins crawled as they bid each other good night and went into their new homes.

Unknown to them, Big Bad Wolf had been watching them in the darkness with fascination. He was shunned by all in the village. The three pigs waved their hooves around instead of talking. Maybe they were different from the villagers.

Big Bad Wolf decided he needed to rest up and could wait until the next day to approach them.

The three pigs left their homes early the next morning to buy some food and supplies, returning home in the afternoon. Big Bad Wolf crouched in wait and watched them from his spot in the forest. He decided the time had come to approach them.

Big Bad Wolf cautiously approached the house of hay, figuring the pig inside would be easy to get to. Big Bad Wolf peered through the window and saw Pig1, who was startled to see him.

"Open the door," Big Bad Wolf asked, knocking on the locked door.

"No, no, not in your lifetime," motioned Pig1 through the window, his heart pounding.

"Okay, then I'll huff and puff and blow your house down!" replied Big Bad Wolf, drawing a deep, deep breath. With that, he huffed and puffed and blew down the house of hay.

Pig1, frightened, raced into Pig2's house, with Big Bad Wolf in hot pursuit. Pig2 slammed the door in Big Bad Wolf's face and double-bolted the door.

"You're safe here," Pig2 said to Pig1. Both peered at Big Bad Wolf through the window and saw him motioning to them to open the door. Suddenly, Big Bad Wolf started banging on the door and yelling, "Open the door!"

"No, no, not in your lifetime," gestured Pig1 and Pig2 through the window, their hearts pounding.

"Okay, then I'll huff and puff and blow your house down!" replied Big Bad Wolf, drawing a deep, deep breath. With that, he huffed and puffed and blew, took another deep, deep breath, huffed and puffed and blew down the house of twigs and sticks.

The two terrified pigs raced next door to Pig3's house, opened the back door, slammed it behind them, and triple-bolted the back and front doors.

"You're really safe here," Pig3 said to Pig1 and Pig2. They pressed their snouts against the window to see what Big Bad Wolf would do next.

"Well, here we go again," Big Bad Wolf thought to himself. "Another house to blow down then I'll have the three pigs," as he sauntered over to the house of bricks.

The three peered at Big Bad Wolf through the window and saw him motioning to them to open the door. He began pounding on the door, yelling, "Open the door!"

"No, no, not in your lifetime," gestured Pig1, Pig2 and Pig3 through the window, their hearts racing.

"Okay, then I'll huff and puff and blow your house down!" replied Big Bad Wolf, drawing a deep, deep breath. With that, he huffed and puffed and blew, took another deep, deep breath, huffed and puffed and blew at the house of bricks. But the house of bricks stood firm. Big Bad Wolf stepped back, drew another big, deep, deep breath and tried again, and again, until he was blue in the face. But he could not budge the house of bricks.

Exasperated, out of breath, and dizzy from huffing and puffing so much, Big Bad Wolf decided to climb quietly up the roof and slide down the chimney into the house. Unknown to Big Bad Wolf, Pig3 had already started a big kettle of soup for dinner, boiling over the fireplace.

The three pigs looked out of all the windows but could see neither hair nor hide of Big Bad Wolf. Deciding that Big Bad Wolf had given up and retreated back into the woods, they started chuckling about beating Big Bad Wolf and thanking Pig3 for saving them with his wise decision to build a sturdy house of bricks. In the meantime, Big Bad Wolf was crawling on their steep roof towards the chimney, also chuckling and envisioning how he'd surprise the three pigs inside their home.

So cocksure was Big Bad Wolf that his strategy would succeed that he began hurrying towards the chimney instead of being careful. He suddenly lost his footing, slid down, and frantically clawed in

vain at the roof to stop his fall. He tumbled down and landed on the ground with an enormous thud, which reverberated throughout the house of brick.

"Did you feel that?" exclaimed Pig3.

"Falling tree?" said Pig1.

"Earthquake?" asked Pig2.

"A meteor?" suggested Pig3.

The three pigs went outside to look and found Big Bad Wolf withering in agony on the ground. Shocked, they asked what happened. Big Bad Wolf moaned and motioned that he had fallen from the roof, and could not get up. His legs were broken.

There Big Bad Wolf lay, in their new garden, as helpless as a baby, as the three pigs looked down at him.

The three pigs, touched by this sorry sight, carried Big Bad Wolf into the house of bricks, put ice on his legs, made splints for his legs, and offered him some warm soup from the kettle. Big Bad Wolf, moved by their kindness, resolved to become friends with them.

"Why'd you pound on the doors and scare us? Why'd you blow our houses down? Why do you want to catch us?" the three pigs demanded.

Big Bad Wolf stared at them and stammered out an explanation, "How else could I get in and visit with you, my new neighbors? You don't have doorbells. You can't hear those. I knocked on the door but you can't hear that, either. What else was I to do?" His eyes looked at them pleadingly.

It was now the three pigs' turn to stare at Big Bad Wolf in disbelief. Big Bad Wolf had wanted to be their friend, and not for them to be his meal! But he had terrified them. What a big, big misunderstanding!

Pig3 remembered that his new friends said that doorbells were part of the village culture. Neighbors rang doorbells to notify homeowners that they were at the door. But how could Deaf homes use doorbells?

"I know!" Pig2 piped up. "We can rig a light, one that will flash when the doorbell rings." Pig2 said he would make something like that and so he did.

So that was how it came to pass that the house of brick had a fine doorbell that flashed a lamp to alert residents if somebody was at the door. The lamp bulb changed colors depending on how the doorbell was rung or who rang it.

Animals from miles around came to marvel at this amazing invention and to buy the light kit from the three pigs. It didn't matter if they were Deaf or not; the visitors liked the novelty of the rainbow colors.

Next door, Pig1 established an awesome bakery. On the other side of the brick house, Pig2 built and ran a shop where housewares and gadgets were sold. Pig3 opened up a coffeehouse and bookstore where he also tutored students. When the animals came to see the marvelous rainbow lights, they could also buy some rolls, coffee, books and gadgets.

> HERE-HERE, HOME-HOME-HOME
> HERE-HERE, PERFECT-PERFECT-PERFECT
> FRIENDS-FRIENDS, MANY-MANY-MANY
> HERE-HERE, STAY-STAY-STAY!

As the pigs signed, their heads swayed back and forth in rhythm with their signs.

Big Bad Wolf learned how to sign and became good friends with the three pigs. He made it clear to other wolves in the forest that the three pigs were his friends. Floating lights at night no longer terrified the three pigs. And they lived happily ever after.

BAT, BIRDS, AND BEASTS

 great conflict was about to start between the Deaf Birds and the Hearing Beasts. They argued and argued for days, but could not arrive at a solution. One day, they decided to declare war on each other.

Bat was not sure which army to join.

The Birds flew by his perch and said, "Join us!"

But Bat shook his head no and said, "I am a Hard of Hearing Bat. I can hear and talk."

The Beasts walked by, looked up, and saw Bat hanging from a limb. They said, "Join us!"

But Bat said, "I am a Hard of Hearing Bat. I don't always understand what you say."

Fortunately, a few hours before the war started, the leaders of the two armies came together to discuss solutions. After they realized the Birds and the Beasts were more alike than different, they decided to call the war off. They signed a declaration supporting peace, respect, and equality for all animals, and then they went home to celebrate.

Bat went to the Birds and asked to join their celebrations. But the Birds said, "You are not one of us. Go away."

Bat went to the Beasts and asked to join their celebrations. But the Beasts said, "You are not one of us. Go away."

Bat was sad because he did not belong to either group. Neither group accepted him.

The next day, both the Birds and the Beasts had a celebration together. Bat decided to approach them again and asked to join them.

The Bird Leader and the Beast Leader looked at him and said, "Are you Bird or Beast? Are you Deaf or Hearing?"

"I don't know, but I have a mind and a heart just like you all," Bat said. "I want to be friends with you all."

The two leaders looked at each other, and responded, "Yes, you are right. We value diversity and respect within our kingdom. Will you vow to do that too?"

"Yes!" Bat promised. He was overjoyed as the Birds and the Beasts welcomed him, and smiled at his new friends. Everyone laughed and chatted in any way they could.

MORAL: Community includes unity and differences.

THE PRINCESS AND
THE 20 MATTRESSES

n the faraway land of Fingermore, Deaf, hard of hearing, DeafBlind, and hearing citizens lived together and mingled effortlessly. Their varying hearing levels were accepted as part of the human variety, much like different eye, hair, and skin colors. The official languages there were Fingermore Sign Language (FSL) for communications and the alphabetized version of FSL for reading and writing. They also knew a third language, English, which was important to keep up with developments in other countries, since international newspapers, documents and books were published in English.

Fingermore was a very Deaf-friendly and people-friendly country. All schools used FSL to communicate, read and write. Fingermore students excelled in school, and when they graduated they went to universities or got good jobs, or both. The country was fully accessible, with Deaf, hard of hearing, Deaf-Plus and hearing people collaborating in schools, markets, and community programs.

The Fingermore Royal family ruled the land. They were Deaf, and all of their royal ancestors were Deaf. Since they were royalty, they had to make sure that their children, who would become kings, queens, and heirs, inherited pure Deaf blood and were Deaf. This meant that they heard absolutely nothing. The less one could hear, the more pure one's Deaf royal blood was. Pure Deaf blood brought one inner peace and wisdom, and was a highly sought characteristic in royal circles.

Prince was ready to marry. When he married, he would become king of Fingermore. The maiden he selected to marry had to show that she was qualified to become the queen. She had to be Deaf, with pure Deaf royal blood in her. She also had to be wise, kind, and Deaf-centered. That meant she must exhibit an intrinsic understanding of being Deaf and know about the Deaf community, history, language and culture. She had to be literate and fluent in FSL and English.

Prince visited royal families in other lands to seek a wife. Prince searched high and low, but he could not find a maiden who possessed the characteristics expected of a queen. He returned to the Fingermore palace in despair. His parents insisted he continue to search until he found a true Deaf blood maiden who was wise, kind, Deaf-centered, and fluent in FSL and English.

Prince continued to search, but in vain. Weeks passed.

Late afternoon on one dark stormy, rainy day, the palace torches on the walls flickered wildly. This meant someone was at the door. A servant answered the door, and there stood a maiden; her clothes were drenched through to the skin. She signed, "I was riding my horse when the skies opened up, it rained, and lighting struck my horse. I am a princess. I kindly request a place to stay tonight."

The servant went to the queen to inform her of the surprise visitor who claimed to be a Deaf princess.

Queen's eyebrows rose. "Princess? Yes, show her in! Have her sit in the library. We will join her shortly."

Queen called King, Prince and Princess. She said to them, "A Deaf maiden has just arrived at our door. She claims to be a princess. She was caught in the rain, and needs a place to stay overnight. Let's meet her and secretly give her the true blood royal Deaf test. I'll ask the Royal FSL and English Proficiency Interviewer to pose as a servant and secretly assess her language skills."

The family gathered in the library to meet the wet maiden. She was drying herself by the roaring fireplace. An attractive maiden, she had dark curly locks, long eyelashes, and slender, long fingers. She was dressed very nicely, with a full, billowing riding dress and fine leather handmade boots. Was she really a true blood Deaf princess? They'd see.

When the maiden saw them, she stood up and curtsied deeply. After introductions, Prince was instantly smitten with her. He thought to himself, "I hope she passes the test!" Tea, scones, and fruits were served.

"Where are you from and where are you going on this rainy afternoon?" they asked.

"I'm Rita Jenna from the Handsmore family in Handsmore country. I decided to explore the neighboring woods on horseback. Suddenly the skies opened up and then lightning struck my horse. I had to walk two hours to get to the Fingermore Town Center. I am grateful that even though we have never met, you are kind enough to allow me to stay overnight."

"Oh, but of course," answered Queen. Please do join us for dinner. We can continue to chat until bedtime."

"I'd love that," responded Rita Jenna.

During dinner, they exchanged news and stories. Rita Jenna shared stories about her family and her country, Handsmore, and how similar Handsmore seemed to be to Fingermore in community, culture, and sign language. She wanted to learn more about Fingermore. As the evening wore on, they discovered that they knew some of the same people and had some of the same experiences. Rita Jenna and Prince sat next to each other, and seemed to enjoy each other's company.

Over dessert, King told a story, as he usually did near the end of dinner.

Once upon a time, a queen sent a scientist and two soldiers to explore a faraway land. Her great ships sailed halfway around the world to a jungle near an inactive volcano. The group foraged deep into the jungle in search of ancient ruins and treasures. Suddenly a small chimpanzee, wearing an ancient gold necklace, dashed in front of the scientist and two soldiers. The scientist got excited and ran after the chimp with the two soldiers chasing her. Soon, they realized that they were hopelessly lost—and the chimp was nowhere to be seen.

Suddenly the ground rumbled. Trees swayed and the group saw gorillas as big as trees running past them. The trio quickly hid in a cave and tried to decide what to do. They were spellbound as they observed the gorillas from the cave. The gorillas plucked fruits from top of the trees, sat around and conversed in sign language. Females were cuddling and feeding their babies while male gorillas brought food and watched for intruders. The lost explorers marveled at how human-like the gorillas acted.

Pretty soon it grew dark. The trio decided to wait until the sun rose the next morning. They could then walk eastward towards the sun to the shore, where they would surely be rescued. Early the next morning, they crept among the bushes, trying not to disturb the gorillas.

Unfortunately, the gorillas were also up and about, foraging for food. One espied the three humans, who began to run for their lives. But the gorilla easily swooped them up and examined them as they cringed in his massive hand, held high above the ground. He was fascinated by the lovely scientist and held on to her as he flung the soldiers away.

King looked around the table. His family and Rita Jenna were enthralled with the story. "Please go on!" they pleaded.

"Alright," King said.

The gorilla looked at the lovely scientist and asked her to marry him."

Everyone was sitting at the edge of their seats. Rita Jenna asked, "And then?"

King looked at Rita Jenna and smiled. "No. I want you to finish the story."

Rita Jenna looked around the table, but the others did not answer. She thought and then said, "When the gorilla asked the scientist to marry him, he accidentally squashed her when he signed MARRY."

"Yes, absolutely right," chuckled King. The family smiled approvingly.

Queen thought, "So far, so good." Rita Jenna had passed the language competency interview and the Deaf-centric wisdom test. Two more areas to go: the kindness and the Deaf royal blood tests. She said, "Well, it is getting late. We better get ready for bed. Rita Jenna, you will sleep in the princess's bedroom. She can sleep in Grandma's room."

"Oh no your majesty," protested Rita Jenna, "the room belongs to Princess and I don't want her to give it up. I will be happy to sleep in any of the servants' rooms."

"Oh no, it is perfectly fine," responded Princess with a brave smile, as she hid her true feelings about being displaced for the night. "It's indeed the most comfortable and prettiest room in the palace!"

"Oh, well, if you are sure you don't mind. That is really very nice of you," Rita Jenna said.

Queen winked secretly at Princess. Rita Jenna had passed the kindness and humility test.

Queen led Rita Jenna to her bedroom for the night, gave her a nightgown, told her the time breakfast would be served, bid her a good night's sleep, and left the room.

Rita Jenna's eyes opened wide as she saw the room. It was truly beautiful. There were roses in vases everywhere. The large four-

post bed supported a stack of twenty mattresses, and was topped by a pink canopy. She had to use a ladder to get to the top. She climbed up, pulled the blanket around her, snuggled in, fluffed the pillows, and got ready to sleep.

But Rita Jenna did not feel comfortable. She tossed and turned. Minutes turned into hours. Still, she tossed and turned and gasped for breath. She felt like gagging. She could not sleep. Finally, the sun came up. She washed herself, brushed her hair, dressed, and went to meet the royal family for breakfast.

"Good morning, Rita Jenna. Did you have a good night's sleep?" inquired Queen. The family's eyes were all on her as they anxiously awaited her answer.

Rita Jenna wanted to be polite and answer "Yes," but she could not lie. "Oh, the room was beautiful and cozy. However for some reason, I could not sleep. I turned and tossed all night. I also was gasping for air and gagging. I do not know why. Maybe I am allergic to something in the room," she said wearily with a polite smile.

King, Queen, Prince, and Princess jumped up, laughing, crying, cheering and waving their hands in the air.

Rita Jenna stared at them in disbelief and thought, "Why are they happy I suffered so much?"

Prince walked up to Rita Jenna, and said, "Rita Jenna, you have proven yourself to be a true blood Deaf Princess!" Queen embraced her and explained, "We are really sorry that we put you through such misery. But to prove that you are a true blood Deaf Princess with a Deaf center, we had to put you through this test. At the bottom of the 20 mattresses we put a wooden tongue depressor. Only a true blood Deaf-centered Princess would be sensitive to the tongue depressor, toss, turn and gag."

Rita Jenna immediately understood. When she was a little girl, her speech teacher often used a wood tongue depressor to teach her how to correctly make the "k" and "g" sounds. But she often gagged with that depressor in her mouth. No wonder she could feel it through all those mattresses! A smile overtook the look of dismay on her face.

Prince held both of Rita Jenna's hands in his hands tenderly, "Please marry me. Our future is in your hands, darling. And I promise I'll never squash you!" Both broke out in laughter and embraced each other.

THE EMPEROR'S CLOTHES

nce upon a time, there lived an emperor who was kind and fair—a fine gentleman. He also struggled with his speech, no matter how hard he practiced. He had difficulties presenting to audiences. To boost his self-confidence and esteem, he made sure he was always well-dressed. The rooms in his palace were filled with exquisite and expensive clothes made from the finest silks and gold threads, sewn by extremely skilled weavers and tailors, from all over the world. The fabrics for his clothes were woven with intricate designs reserved for royalty.

In spite of his fine clothes, he avoided giving public speeches whenever he could. His advisors encouraged him to find alternate means of communication, but the emperor refused to try anything else. After all, he was the emperor and did not need to do anything he did not want to do. When it was absolutely necessary to present, the Emperor had the Royal Enunciator repeat a few of his key statements during his presentations.

Everyone knew about the emperor's love for fine clothes and his speech challenges. Everyone accepted the emperor's quirks because he was a very kind emperor who treated people fairly and kept peace with neighboring countries.

One day, in a distant land across an ocean, Mr. Bell, a swindler, learned about this emperor's love for fancy and expensive clothes. Bell decided to visit the emperor and sell him the Bell line of clothes. He announced himself as the proprietor of the Bell Tailor Shop, a prize-winning designer of fine clothes. The emperor, intrigued, welcomed Bell into his palace and was quite impressed with the sketches of magnificent clothes and cloaks produced by the Bell Tailor Shop, Limited.

Bell proposed, "I will make you something even better! This exotic garment will be woven, sewn and fitted for only you. Moreover, it will have magical powers. First, only smart people will be able to see it. The fabric will be invisible to anyone who is dumb. You will see the difference in intelligence of your subjects when you wear it. Second, it will give you the power of fluent speech. People will understand you easily. If they don't, they are dumb."

The emperor exclaimed, "Really?! I must have that garment! Not only do I want to be the best dressed person in the land, I also want to speak clearly. Speech practice does not help me. I also want to know who is smart and who is not."

"Certainly," smiled Bell. "Just sign on the dotted line. The outfit will be ready in two months. You can send someone to my shop every week to inspect the progress. You must pay me on a weekly basis. This is how much will be payable, per week." Bell showed the emperor the contract.

The emperor gasped when he saw the amount. It was practically a king's ransom. However, he wanted so much to be elegantly dressed, to speak clearly and to know who was smart and who was dumb. He signed the contract. The emperor's advisors were skeptical and looked at him quizzically by giving side-eye looks, but dared not to question him.

"Thank you," said Bell with a big smile on his face, as he backed out of the emperor's huge room, bowing while clutching the contract carefully in his hands.

Bell set up a secret shop on the outskirts of the town that was closed to the public. It had no windows. He put in looms of varying sizes, and people walking by could hear the looms humming and spinning.

An emperor's advisor visited the shop to investigate the progress and to make the first weekly payment. Bell welcomed him into his shop.

"Ah, I've just begun. Do you like what you see?" asked Bell, confidently with a big smile on his face. His arms were outstretched. He pointed confidently to the different looms.

The emperor's advisor looked around him, and saw looms humming and spinning. But he did not see anything come out of the looms. He rubbed his eyes, put on his spectacles, and looked again, but still saw nothing. Fearful of being identified as dumb, he replied, "Yes, I see the creation of threads. They are lovely." He paid Bell and left the shop. He reported to the emperor that the work had started and it was going well. The emperor was pleased with the first progress report.

And so it went. Every week the emperor sent an advisor to review progress at the shop, to make the weekly payment, and to report back to him. Each week, a new kind of machine was added. One week, it was a weaving machine that went *thimp-thump* as the weft pick shuttled horizontally across the vertical warps. Two weeks later, a threading machine was added. It went *whirl, whirl, whirl* as it threaded. The following week, a sewing machine made zig-zagging motions. The next week, a button-fastening machine was looping in and out.

Each week, each advisor could not see any fabrics or threads at all. But each feared being labeled dumb, so he always bit his tongue and exclaimed how beautiful the material was and how well the work was progressing. Each week Bell received his huge payment. He was already making plans to run away as soon as the outfit was finished. He would live far away, be a wealthy landowner, and live happily ever after. He also planned to make deals with wealthy families who had children wanting to learn speech to create magical robes for them so they could speak clearly and be smart.

The emperor, delighted with the positive weekly reports from his advisors, proclaimed that there would be a special ceremony when the garment was ready. Everyone from near and far would be invited to partake in the ceremony and the feast. The emperor would show off his magnificent new garment and make a presentation to his people about his accomplishments and his master plan for the future of his beloved country and his people.

The palace hummed as his servants prepared for the huge ceremony. Everyone was excited to see the emperor's new robe and to hear his plans.

The emperor worked enthusiastically on writing his presentation. For the first time, he would deliver it all by himself, unaided, instead of having the Royal Enunciator repeat some sentences. For this reason, his plan for the future needed to be as bold, far-reaching, and inspiring as the unveiling of his new robe and his new speech skills.

Finally the much-anticipated day arrived. Bell came to the palace that morning. The emperor and all his advisors greeted him warmly. With much fanfare, Bell opened the large package containing the outfit, enclosed in several layers of tissue paper. The emperor impatiently wished there were not so many layers of tissue paper. The last layer was finally removed, and Bell handed the robe gingerly to the emperor.

"It is magnificent, is it not?" exclaimed Bell proudly as the emperor examined the robe. "Now, please undress and put on the robe so that I can make any needed adjustments before you go to the ceremony."

The Emperor blinked. He could see nothing. His advisors around him made oohing and aahing expressions about the robe. He said, "Yes, indeed, it is exquisite. We have never seen anything like this before."

The emperor swallowed hard and put on the robe. He did not want to be seen as dumb because he could not see or feel the robe. "Yes, it fits perfectly," he said as he viewed himself in the mirror. His advisors looked at each other because the emperor's speech was still not clear. But they remained polite and silent because they feared they would be considered dumb. Two servants appeared to carry the robe train behind him. The emperor decided he now had better focus on his presentation and stepped outside.

The crowd awaited the arrival of the emperor with much enthusiasm. They could not wait to see his much-heralded new garment, which could distinguish smart people from dumb people. They could not wait for him to deliver, all by himself, his presentation on the future of their country. The emperor paraded from the palace to the town center toward the stage. His servants were in front of him, strewing red rose petals on the red carpet. Two servants behind him held the train of his robe. The emperor smiled and waved to his people.

The crowd throbbed as people craned their necks to see. What they saw puzzled them, but they dared not to say anything, lest they appear dumb.

Royal trumpets sounded and heralds waved in the air. The emperor took his place on the stage. With much fanfare, the emperor fiddled a bit with the loudspeaker horn and began his presentation, "Ladies and gentlemen, it gives me much pleasure…"

The townsfolk did not know what to make of this apparent farce. Finally, the polite silence and pretended admiration of the crowd was shattered when a small child blurted out, "The emperor has on no clothes!"

Another child exclaimed, "We can't understand the emperor at all."

The townsfolk looked at the children and then at each other. They admitted, "Yes, the children speak the truth."

The townsfolk started pointing at the emperor and said that they did not understand him. They gestured that they could not see any clothes on the emperor. The emperor stopped his presentation, mortified.

After a moment of silence, one villager said, "Emperor, we love you the way you are!"

A chorus of agreement came from the crowd. "Your ideas and actions are magnificent," another said.

"You don't need fancy clothes."

"You don't need to speak to get your ideas across to us. You can use sign language and interpreters. That can be part of our future plans." The crowd seemed to pulsate with relief and faith, now that the truth was out.

The emperor looked at the crowd and realized that he had been duped. He also realized he was fortunate to have such wonderful, loyal subjects. He resolved to put his money into bilingual education for everyone instead of squandering it all on fancy clothes.

"Give me some clothes," he asked his servants, "and let's begin the feast now," he gestured to the crowd.

Led by the Royal Drummer, the crowd erupted into cheers and clapping:

> CLAP, CLAP – CLAP, CLAP, CLAP!
> YOU'RE CHAMP – CHAMP, CHAMP, CHAMP!
> CLAP, CLAP – CLAP, CLAP, CLAP!
> CELEBRATE – CELEBRATE, CELEBRATE, CELEBRATE!
> CLAP, CLAP – CLAP, CLAP, CLAP!
> LOVE YOU – LOVE, LOVE, LOVE!
> CLAP, CLAP – CLAP, CLAP, CLAP!

THREE LITTLE KITTENS

The three little kittens, they wore mittens,
They got home and began to cry,
"Oh, Mother dear, we won't lie,
We must wear mittens."
"What? Were you naughty kittens?
Then you shall have no pie."
"Meow, meow, meow."
"Then you shall have no pie."

The three little kittens, they wore their mittens,
And they continued to cry,
"Oh, Mother dear, see here, see here,
We must wear our mittens.
Teacher said mittens will stop signing."
"What? Signing makes you smart kittens.
Take them off and have some pie."
"Purr, purr, purr,
Oh, let us have some pie."

The three little kittens put away their mittens,
And soon ate up the pie,
"Oh, Mother dear, we must pause,
For we have soiled our paws."
"What, soiled your paws, you naughty kittens!"
Then they began to sigh,
"Meow, meow, meow,"
Then they began to sigh.

The three little kittens, they washed their paws,
And polished their claws,
"Oh, Mother dear, open your eyes,
We have washed our paws
And polished our claws."
"What, washed your paws, then you're good kittens,
I smell Teacher close by."
"Meow, meow, meow."
"I smell Teacher close by.
Pull in your claws."

THREE ORAL MICE

Three oral mice. Three oral mice.
See how they run. See how they run.
They all ran after the Deaf Baby's Mother.
The Mother they did bother,
With their squeaky voice,
"Signing is a freaky choice,
Signing is a wacky choice!"

The Deaf Baby's Mother scolded them,
"I know what's best for my baby.
About that, there's no maybe.
Get lost or I'll give you real strife,
I'll chop off your tails with a knife."
See how they ran for dear life?
Did you ever see such a tale in your life
As three oral mice, three oral mice?

THE TORTOISE
AND THE HARE

By Suzy Rosen Singleton

nce upon a time many centuries ago in a fantastic land that no longer exists, there was a village of talking animals whose conduct and behavior were strikingly similar to that of humans. The animals in this village lived in houses, had full-time jobs, and created flourishing schools to educate their young. This village buzzed with much happiness and productivity as the animals filled their lives with rewarding alliances to build successful businesses, schools, shopping malls, and swimming pools. The village was surrounded by bucolic pastures and charming forests with burbling brooks, around which millions of butterflies and birds fluttered and basked in the pleasant sunny weather.

The story, however, is not about the village, but about a very unlikely friendship between two animals: the tortoise and the hare. Tortoise, sweet with a quiet disposition, was known for being a patient and hard worker. He was always happy to give the many smaller animals rides to and from different places. Standing three feet tall on his back legs, Tortoise's strong, checkered dark olive green shell was pleasing to the touch. His plump green face crinkled when he smiled, and everyone around him couldn't help but smile along with him. His skin felt like softened leather, which lent him an air of kindness and comfort.

Hare was quite the opposite. At nearly six feet, Hare stood tall with erect and long slender ears that moved constantly even though he could not hear the loudest of sounds. Outfitted with a beautiful coat of soft creamy brown fur, the hare was limber, svelte, and quick on his feet. The animals loved to see the hare showcase his speed and bounce, and they roared with laughter at such entertainment.

Tortoise and Hare were a study in contrasts. Along with their heights, Tortoise had a smooth, hard shell; Hare had soft downy fur. Tortoise plodded along; Hare could easily run circles around anyone. Tortoise was careful and humble; Hare loved to show off his athletic prowess. Tortoise and Hare were unlikely best friends, but they were the only Deaf teenagers in the village.

Indeed, they spent much of their leisure time together by themselves, lying out in the sun for hours signing up a storm in Animal Sign Language (ASL). They had so much fun chatting about news, jokes, and curious matters like the longest word possible (and reader, you know the world's longest word is "smiles," because it has a "mile" within it!).

Other days they would toss around a flying disc, skip pebbles in the brook, or play cards. One particularly lazy day after school, Tortoise and Hare eyed each other mischievously, and challenged each other to an all-day race that would wind through the woods and pastures. They begged their favorite teacher to help them create a route.

"Of course, dear children," signed their teacher, Ms. Baboon, "I would be delighted to help." With a twinkle in her eye, she knew that despite Hare's obvious speed advantage, Tortoise was smart. This would be a fun race for the teenagers to while away the weekend.

"Thanks, Ms. Baboon!" Given identical maps, Tortoise and Hare agreed to meet that upcoming Saturday for their race. "Hare, please don't forget to wear your captioning glasses," warned Tortoise. "We may be in the remote and far-flung parts of the village and it might be hard to understand those who don't know ASL."

Hare grinned and retorted, "Tortoise, we grew up here. All I have to do is to orchestrate a few powerful bounces and I will be at the finish line in a matter of minutes."

Tortoise smiled warmly at his friend's audacity and confidence, and said, "Hare, my trusty shell and feet shall take me to the finish line first, slowly but surely!"

The two friends joined in merry laughter as they walked home to finish their homework. Their lively conversation moved to how sign language allowed them to communicate seamlessly despite Hare's bounces. "How lucky we are," they agreed. "Sign language lets us talk even with our mouths full, and even when we are separated by windows!" Their animated chatter continued nonstop as they meandered their way home.

Saturday arrived, and Tortoise and Hare stood at the starting point near school. They were surprised by the crowd of animals who had gathered to see them off. Ms. Baboon led the crowd with hand-waves to wish them luck. Ms. Meerkat, a local qualified interpreter, brought magic ASL amulets on lanyards. Ms. Meerkat exclaimed that these magic ASL amulets could be activated to create holographic interpreters* if needed during the race. This could be especially helpful, given that there were many forks in the road that they might mistakenly take, especially if they took a road less traveled.

Hare said, "No, ma'am, I shall rely on my powerful bounces to spring to the finish line effortlessly!" Tortoise, however, humbly accepted the offer of assistance, remarking, "Why, Ms. Meerkat. That's such a kind offer. Thank you."

Ms. Meerkat beamed and nodded, and placed the thinly roped lanyard over the tortoise's head and adjusted its length. The

---

*The magic ASL amulet is really cool. This technology allows the ghost-like shape of an interpreter to be beamed by magic light from the ASL amulet and appear whenever you press the amulet button. The holographic interpreter can be invoked to provide interpreting services anywhere, anytime. Earthlings are trying to develop this technology, and perhaps by the time you read this, this technology will be available to you!

magic ASL amulet was in the shape of a purple eye, and looked handsome on the tortoise.

"Not only that," Tortoise said, "I also brought my captioning glasses as a backup resource." Ms. Meerkat and Ms. Baboon chortled with laughter, pleased at Tortoise's preparedness, and shook their heads ever so slightly at Hare's refusal to be as prepared as his friend for a race through foreign territories.

"On your mark, get set, GO!" Ms. Baboon signed.

Hare zipped out of sight within moments. Tortoise waved a final goodbye to the fans and ambled onwards to follow the set course. The fans waved energetically.

A few hours passed. Tortoise had remained steadily on course, with one foot following another dutifully. He spotted Hare sleeping blissfully under a majestic weeping willow situated on a lush carpet of green grass. "Heh, sweet Hare," thought Tortoise, "he wanted to be sure he didn't get to the finish line too soon! But I know my dear friend—sometimes his naps get the best of him."

Tortoise continued on his way. A short while later, he reached a fork in the road. He pulled out his map and consulted with a pig tilling her farm by the road, who confirmed the directions via captions that scrolled inside Tortoise's captioning glasses. "Thank you, Ms. Pig," Tortoise gestured respectfully. "Much obliged." He did not dare to stop to rest as he wanted very much to win this race against his dear yet boastful friend. Tortoise smiled to himself about the idea of victory, knowing how unrealistic it was. Onwards he trudged, for hope was an endless well of inspiration for him.

Meanwhile, Hare remained in deep slumber. Only after a bee landed on his sensitive nose did he awaken with a start. "Oh my," wondered Hare as he stretched his long, slender limbs, "this was such a delicious nap, but I fear that so much time has passed."

He quickly jumped to his feet and peered at the horizon. "The finish line just has to be out there, so I'll take a mighty jump to spirit myself to the end of this race," he thought.

Hare gathered all his might and took a ginormous leap that took him straight up through several layers of puffy clouds, the highest and farthest he had ever leaped to date! When he landed, he could not figure out where he was. Surrounded by many statuesque trees, he saw a multitude of paths that would take him in every direction.

"Why," thought Hare, "I'm truly lost!" He wanted to use the map, but realized he had neglected to pack it. He ran into Ms. Moose, who tried to help him, but Hare had no captioning glasses or magic amulet to communicate — unlike his friend Tortoise. Hare also could not understand Mr. Woodpecker and Mr. Butterfly, as much as they wanted to help him.

Hare lamented his lack of foresight in bringing the glasses and amulet, sinking in his brooding thoughts. He had no choice but to continue to zip and bounce through the thick of the forest, remaining as lost as ever. He started to get frightened and disoriented, and continued to bounce from one incomprehensible animal to another.

The sun began to set. Tortoise was still inching his way to the finish line. He looked at his magic ASL amulet and saw holographic ASL translations of the crowd's praise and encouragement, which cheered him onwards to the finish line. "Where is Hare?" Tortoise wondered to himself. "I should expect to see him anytime now!" He gingerly stepped across the finish line, and was declared the victor as he was raised in the air by the many cheering animals awaiting him.

Despite his joy, Tortoise was worried. "Say, have you seen my friend, Hare?" Mr. Donkey voiced his signs, and a sea of shaking heads answered him.

Hare, finally resigned to his fate, took a mighty backwards leap and landed back on the road near the beginning of the race. He spotted the school. Lo and behold, there was Ms. Baboon, who was rushing back to the school to call for a search and rescue team.

"Ms. Baboon!" Hare signed, tearful and relieved.

"I was so frightened! And now here you are!" Ms. Baboon shrieked with happiness and quickly took Hare via a short cut to the finish line, where Tortoise anxiously remained in wait for his friend.

"Tortoise, my dear friend," exclaimed Hare, "your victory is well deserved. Congratulations!"

Tortoise let out a huge sigh of relief, and said, "Hare, my dear friend. We are both winners because we are best friends. How happy I am that you are safe!"

Hare nodded his head vigorously and said, "Tortoise, I agree. I have learned my lesson to be as prepared as I can be for any challenge. For that invaluable lesson, I thank you."

The friends hugged each other warmly, and the crowd erupted in cheers at their sportsmanship. The racers broke into great laughter. "I just had a bad hare day," Hare joked. The crowd marveled as they watched Tortoise and Hare walk away together, arm in arm, challenging each other to yet another race 'morrow.

THE LITTLE MERMAID

nce upon a time, in the depths of the sea, there was a royal castle made of stones, reeds, and shells along with pearls and other jewels of the sea. The floor of the turquoise-colored sea seemed magical, lit by rays of sunlight from above and carpeted with flowers and plants that swayed gracefully with the sea's gentle rocking motions.

In the castle lived Sea King with his five daughters, all mermaids. Sea people have strong, graceful fish-like tails. The sea people all were fluent in sign language, which was essential for communicating underwater. Sea King's mother, also a mermaid, took care of the sea princesses. They all were beautiful girls with bright eyes, shimmering fishtails, and long tresses of red hair that waved underwater. The prettiest of them all was the youngest princess, Little Mermaid. When she signed, it was pure poetry for the eyes. Everyone from everywhere in the sea kingdom came to see her sign songs and sonnets; they could watch her perform forever, especially with her tresses flowing like an aura around her, her fishtail gently waving, and the flowers and reeds swaying in tune behind her. The flowing and ebbing motions created a visual symphony.

Mermaids live three hundred years, and at the end of their lives, they turn into sea foam. When a mermaid reaches the age of fifteen, she is permitted to go above water and observe the moon, constellations of stars, ships, trees, and people—but only at night. Mermaids must remain unseen by human eyes.

Little Mermaid loved Grandma's tales about the upper world, and pestered her to tell more stories. One story remained in Little Mermaid's thoughts, and she could not shake it loose. Grandma said that humans had short life spans, but then their souls went to heaven. Sea people on the other hand, although they lived for three hundred years, turned into sea foam.

"Grandma," asked Little Mermaid with a pout, "why can't we have souls and go to heaven, too? It isn't fair."

"Well, if you marry someone who holds you dearer than anything else in the world, part of his soul will flow into you," Grandma explained. "But that's not possible for mermaids." She saw Little Mermaid's face cloud, and smiled. "But who knows?"

Little Mermaid turned fifteen and was finally allowed to surface briefly, but only when the moonlight was beginning to shine or to fade. Little Mermaid was fascinated with passing ships and the hustle and bustle on their decks. She noticed that people on the ships were moving around, and their tails seemed to be split in half, which helped them to move around. Her older sisters laughed when she shared her observation. They explained that humans did not have tails; they had legs and feet, which were like arms and hands except that they were affixed below the torso.

"Can their legs sign too?" asked the wide-eyed Little Mermaid.

"No," chortled her sisters, "they talk with their mouths instead of with their hands."

One night, Little Mermaid sat on a rock, her eyes transfixed on a grand ship. She suddenly saw with horror that one of the men had fallen overboard. He hit a rock and was floating, face down, unconscious. Little Mermaid quickly swam over to him, and with her free hand, towed him to safety on the shore. She breathed air back into him. The moonlight lit up his face; he was strikingly handsome. Little Mermaid recognized him as the prince of the land kingdom. She made sure he was safe, and swam away quickly before other people arrived to rescue him. She couldn't be seen by human eyes.

After that, Little Mermaid could not keep her mind off Prince. She yearned to be with him. Her family implored her to forget him. After all, Little Mermaid and Prince were from different worlds, and there was no way they could be together on land or in sea. But Little Mermaid was as strong-minded as she was beautiful. She could not be persuaded to forget Prince.

After days of longing, she decided to visit the Sea Witch to see if the Sea Witch could grant her legs.

With legs, she could go on shore and be with Prince. She was sure she would win his heart. At the very least she could be close to him.

Sea Witch said, "Do you realize that when you get your legs, you cannot go back to being a mermaid? If you do not marry Prince within six months, you will die and become sea foam. Do you still want those legs?"

Little Mermaid exclaimed, "Oh yes, anything! I want to be near him and I am sure he will want to be with me, too."

"There is a price to pay, you know," cackled Sea Witch. "Like everyone else, I admire and desire your signing beauty. The price for your new legs is that I will acquire your beautiful sign language ability and you will be left mute, unable to sign anymore."

"Yes, yes, I agree," Little Mermaid signed, biting her lip and hesitating ever so slightly. "Anything for legs."

"One more thing," continued Sea Witch, "walking on feet will be painful for you."

"Anything for legs," Little Mermaid persisted, with an affirmative nod.

"Very well," said Sea Witch, guffawing. "Tonight when the moon is out, go forth to shore. When you reach the shore, your fishtail will transform into legs. You cannot ever become a mermaid again. If Prince marries anyone else, you will turn into sea foam."

Little Mermaid swam enthusiastically to the sea castle to bid her family farewell. In spite of their admonitions and wailing, Little Mermaid declared that it was a done deed, that she would love her family forever, and that she had to follow her heart. Her heart beat wildly as she swam towards the shore before the moonlight faded. Her eyes shone with excitement.

She landed on shore. She felt her fishtail buzz, sizzle and tingle as it shed the fish scales, split into two, and transformed into legs and feet. She felt like a big bolt of electricity had gone through her body, but now she had legs! She carefully got up and learned how to balance on her feet, holding on to the sea wall for support. She walked a few paces. Her legs were burning, but she would get used to this new sensation.

She walked to the Prince's palace, and stumbled from exhaustion onto the marble steps of the prince's palace.

The sun arose and awakened Little Mermaid. Temporarily blinded by the sun, she shielded her eyes and gradually became accustomed to the bright light of the upper world. She realized she was in a beautiful garden, surrounded by neatly manicured flowers and plants that stood still. She had legs and feet, but no clothes. She quickly wrapped herself with her long hair. Just then, a shadow came over her. She looked up and saw that it was Prince. His dark eyes had an intense look as he helped her to her feet.

"Who are you and what happened?" he asked.

She started to answer, but remembered that she no longer knew sign language. All the signs had been regulated to the dark, deep recesses of her mind, now only a glimmer of a memory. She simply stared at him with doe-like eyes. Prince became concerned, and called his maids to come and take care of her and to provide her with food and clothes.

"Poor girl, she cannot talk," the maids whispered among themselves, "but maybe with our care, she will regain her speech." They let her stay in a bedroom overlooking the sea.

Little Mermaid loved living in the palace, so near her beloved prince.

During the day, she would walk around the garden. Sometimes at night she would sneak to the shore and see her sisters swimming around, and they would update her about her father, grandmother and the family. She could still understand their signs, but they understood she could no longer sign back to them.

Prince came and visited her in the garden daily. She was so beautiful, so radiant, so calm, and so mysterious that Prince was attracted to her. He hoped that if he chatted with her about himself, maybe she would also open up and talk with him. He told her stories of his experiences growing up, his voyages to strange lands, and his family. Little Mermaid could lipread a bit, catching bits and pieces of his dialogue. He told her that once he had fallen overboard and was saved by a young maiden, but her identity was unknown to him. He had been searching for her and when he found her, he would be linked to her forever with gratitude.

Little Mermaid gasped. She had to tell him she was that young maiden. But how? She could not sign, and had no recollection of expressive language. But Little Mermaid was as strong-willed as she was beautiful. She would find a way, she decided.

In the meantime, King informed Prince that since he was now twenty years old, it was time for him to marry. Prince responded that he wanted to first find the maiden who had saved his life. King pointed out that Prince had already wasted too much time searching for her, but Prince had one last place he wanted to search. Around the bend in the mountain, in the next country, was another sea town. King relented and gave Prince one more month.

Little Mermaid recoiled in dismay when Prince told her he had to set sail the following day to find the mystery maiden to marry her. He was pretty sure that sea town around the bend was where he fell overboard and hit his head. Prince reassured Little

Mermaid that he loved her always but that he was committed to finding the maiden who had saved his life.

For days afterwards, Little Mermaid paced around her bedroom. She faced the mirror in her room, her image staring back at her. She thought, "What do I do now?" She drummed her fingers on the dresser, in deep thought. "Aha, I've got it!" she suddenly thought. She started to wiggle her fingers. She then walked her fingers on the dresser. She lifted her hand and waved her hand. She raised her other hand and waved it too. She brought both hands together and clasped them near her heart. Her heart leaped with joy. "Yes, that would work!"

There was much commotion when Prince's ship docked back at the palace. He had a lovely maiden on his arm when he disembarked the ship, a princess from the neighboring sea town and her parents had given her consent to visit Prince's family.

Little Mermaid's heart sank. Not only would she lose the love of her life, she would also lose her life if she didn't do something quickly.

When Prince arrived at the palace, he made a beeline for Little Mermaid, who was, as usual, in her favorite spot on the beach, near the garden.

"I've found the maiden who saved me! And she is a princess too. Now, don't you fret," he said, seeing Little Mermaid's worried face. "You will always live with us. You're very special to me."

Little Mermaid's smile at the sight of Prince transformed into a frown when he said that.

"It's now or never," she thought.

She started to pantomime, a little awkwardly at first, shaking her head and using her hands, her expressions, and her body to say, "No, no. Not her."

Prince was taken aback. Little Mermaid was communicating! What did she mean by, "No, no. Not her?" Was she jealous?

Sign language was hard-wired in Little Mermaid's brain and although it could not be used, it was not completely forgotten. With its foundation firmly rooted in her mind, Little Mermaid pantomimed with increasing flair and clarity.

"Me in water. Saw you fall. Me swim save you. Me bring you to shore. Me blow air in your mouth. Me swim away."

Prince could not believe his eyes. She was the one who saved him! Yes, he vaguely remembered his savior blowing air into his mouth. It was her!

Prince fell to his knees and proposed. Little Mermaid pantomimed her acceptance, but added that he needed to meet her family first. Prince wholeheartedly agreed.

That night, Little Mermaid went to the shore to see her sisters and pantomimed that Prince had asked for her hand in marriage. She also shared her wish that the wedding take place both on land and underwater in the sea castle. Her sisters said it could be done and to meet them the following night.

The following night, the four sisters appeared near the rocks at the edge of the shore, but they looked different. Their long hair was gone! They explained that they had gone to Sea Witch for a magic potion to help Prince to breathe underwater. In exchange, Sea Witch demanded the long locks of their red hair.

Little Mermaid thanked them profusely as they handed her the vial of magic potion.

The next night, Little Mermaid led Prince to the water to meet her family. She pantomimed that they lived in the water, and that her father was Sea King. She explained through pantomime that she and Prince would visit them underwater so that Prince could ask her father for her hand. She knew this was shocking to him, but hoped that he would love her nonetheless.

Prince responded that he loved her with all his heart and soul, no matter what. He said that their hearts and souls were intertwined forever, and that marriage would seal their immortal love. They put flippers on their feet, and Little Mermaid gave Prince a sip of the magic potion. They held hands as they walked into the water, and dove down to her sea castle.

King, Grandma and four sisters awaited Prince. They signed with delight, "Welcome to our sea palace, Prince. We have been watching you and Little Mermaid, and are happy to finally meet you."

Prince stared at their signing. He signed back, "It is my pleasure." Little Mermaid stared at him in surprise. She asked how he knew signs.

"When the soldiers and I seek sunken treasures, we sign to each other underwater. We sign when we are in places where we cannot speak. Signs are mandatory for us," Prince explained.

Sea King chuckled and embraced Prince. "Good for you, son!" he exclaimed. "Let the ceremonies and celebrations begin!"

Prince and Little Mermaid got married again on land, and lived happily ever after in his palace.

Every month, when there was a full moon, they visited her family at the shoreline.

ONE, TWO, I LOOK

One, two	I LOOK
Three, four	WALK DOOR
Five, six	WANT WATER
Seven, eight	$7? OUTRAGEOUS!
Nine, ten	PEEK-THROUGH-KEYHOLE, KNOCK-KNOCK
Eleven, twelve	I-SPY, JUMPING-AROUND
Thirteen, fourteen	FUNNY MONKEY
Fifteen	GOODBYE!

The Deaf community enjoys stories and songs, especially those that play up the features of American Sign Language (ASL). The fingerspelled alphabet lends itself to the creation of many stories based on signs using the handshapes of the alphabet, in alphabetic order. For example, the handshape A could begin a story with the A handshape knocking on a door, B becomes the door, and C becomes the sign for SEARCH, and so on all the way to Z. This can also apply to fingerspelled numbers.

This song, ONE, TWO, I LOOK, was created with the numbers 1-15. Please feel encouraged to seek and enjoy other "ABC" or number songs, or even create your own. To see a demonstration of how to sign this story, visit www.savorywords.com/rozvideo.

BELLING THE CAT

 long time ago, there was a small country where animals lived together and governed themselves.

One day, a household of Rabbits adopted a cat. Cat liked living with the Rabbits, and did his share of helping around the house. One way Cat did that was by catching mice.

Deaf Mice often gathered together to discuss issues that made their lives difficult. They agreed that their top threat was Cat, because Cat loved to watch Deaf Mice—especially those who used sign language. The movement of their paws as they talked fascinated, yet repulsed, Cat. After watching them, Cat would pounce on the signing mice and eat them. The mice were terrified of Cat. They felt oppressed by Cat. They felt they couldn't move around freely, get food, attend schools, or get jobs because of their fear of Cat.

The Deaf Mice agreed that the biggest problem was the sly way Cat would sneak up on them and catch them. Many ideas were shared at a town hall forum, which was filled with Deaf Mice of all ages and colors from all over:

"Maybe we should stop signing, because we all know that Cat hates sign language. That's why Cat wants to eat us."

"Maybe we should sign only in our rooms behind closed doors."

"Maybe we should turn off the light when we sign. But then how can we see each other?"

"Maybe we should move away from this house."

"Maybe we should get a dog!"

Each idea was considered but then discarded as impractical. After much discussion, a young mouse, Sheri, said she had an idea that would stop Cat from terrorizing the mice. " We should put a bell on Cat so if he approaches, our wristwatch alarm system will go off."

Heads nodded vigorously in agreement as the mice cheered. "Yes, yes!" They applauded by waving their paws in the air.

An old mouse stood up and exclaimed, "Great idea. Now, who will put the bell on Cat?"

The silence in the room was uncomfortable. Not one mouse volunteered to do it. Many were trembling, hoping they wouldn't be randomly selected.

"See!" continued the old mouse. "It is easy to propose impossible solutions. This will never work!"

"No," retorted Sheri, not willing to swallow the bitter pill of defeat. "We can collaborate and do this." She thought of the famous leader Margaret Mouse, and quoted Margaret: "Just a few committed mice can help change the world. In fact, that is the only thing that ever has!"

The mice started nodding their heads, and Sheri continued, "We have the right to life, liberty, and opportunities."

Everyone cheered in agreement.

"Okay, what's the plan?" asked the old mouse, rolling his eyes and waiting for the next outlandish idea.

"We can contact the mayor's office in town about Cat's inhuman deprivation of our rights, sign language, and freedom of movement," Sheri suggested. "We are protected by the Animals with Disabilities Act. The Citizen Protection Program can send police dogs to verify our situation and then require Cat to wear a bell."

Everyone agreed that Sheri's strategy was the best idea and they should do that. And so they did.

MORAL: Know how to pursue your rights, liberty, and opportunities.

HANSEL AND GRETEL

nce upon a time there lived in the forest a poor woodcutter, his wife, and his two children, Hansel and little Gretel. The children's mother had died when they were very young. Woodcutter went to the country fair to seek a wife for himself and a mother for his children. The woman was plain-looking, but she said she could cook and sew and she would help around the house and raise the children. The woodcutter was glad because now he could spend more time cutting and selling wood. Life would improve for them.

Everyone rejoiced when the new wife and stepmother joined the family. Woodcutter said, "This is Hansel and little Gretel." Hansel bowed politely and Gretel curtsied nicely as they signed, "Welcome home."

Stepmother's face fell when she saw them signing. "You didn't tell me they're Deaf! And that they sign!" she yelled at Woodcutter. "That is disgusting!"

Woodcutter responded, "That is how we communicate. They are smart and they are sweet."

"But they still can't talk. I will have no such nonsense in my house! Sign language is forbidden in our country. They must learn to talk and to listen!" she retorted haughtily.

Hansel and Gretel shivered when they lipread those harsh words.

"We can talk some, but not everyone understands us," they said, trying to placate Stepmother, "Signing is clear and natural for us."

"That's not the way it's done in the world," snorted Stepmother. "If I catch you signing, I will beat your hands with a stick. You must use your ear horns all the time to help you listen."

So that is how it came to be that signing was no longer allowed in their home. Hansel and Gretel had to hide their signing. They signed only if Stepmother was out of eyeshot. Otherwise they would get a beating. They wore their ear horns with strings around their necks and pretended to use them and acted as if the ear horns helped.

Woodcutter worked hard at cutting and selling wood, but it was a very difficult way to make a living. His meager earnings brought only a little bit of food to the table for the family. The shady yard did not yield a good crop of vegetables, and their cow died. Some berries grew on bushes in the woods, but as the days went by, there were fewer and fewer berries. A loaf of bread needed to last a few days for the whole family.

One day, Stepmother said to Woodcutter, "We do not have enough food. We will all starve to death. The only way we can survive is if we get rid of Hansel and Gretel."

"Oh no, we cannot do that," responded Woodcutter in horror. "They are my children and I love them."

"It's either starve or get rid of Hansel and Gretel," said Stepmother adamantly. She stood her ground. Finally after days of being henpecked about this, Woodcutter gave in.

Hansel and Gretel had watched their parents argue through a knothole in the wall. They did not understand but knew that something awful might happen.

At dinnertime, they shared a bit of bread and an apple. Stepmother informed Hansel and Gretel that the next morning the family would go in the woods to gather some berries.

Gretel signed to Hansel, "I don't trust her. I'm afraid." Hansel replied that he felt the same way, but he had a plan. At night when everyone was sleeping, Hansel took Gretel's hand and went outside near the creek where round, shiny pebbles nearly outnumbered the twinkling stars above. Hansel and Gretel gathered as many pebbles as they could and put them in their pockets.

The next day, the entire family set out for the woods. Stepmother gave them a half loaf of bread and told them to make it last all day. As they walked deeper and deeper in the woods, Hansel quietly dropped a shiny pebble on the path, every twenty steps or so. After hours of walking, Woodcutter and Stepmother told the children to sit for a while and rest while they continued to forage for berries.

The children sat and waited. They nibbled on the bread. The sun approached the end of its daily orbit. Shadows grew longer and longer. The woods grew darker and darker. Stars started to come out and twinkle. Gretel signed to Hansel, "Maybe they are not coming back."

Hansel replied, "I don't think they're coming back. So let's go home." They got up and followed the path of the round shiny pebbles, which were illuminated by the moon above. They made their way home.

"Hansel and Gretel!" shrieked Stepmother, "what are you doing here?"

"Hansel and Gretel!" yelped Woodcutter with a gulp in his throat, "what a relief."

"You go to bed now!" commanded Stepmother.

Through the knothole in the wall, the children again witnessed Stepmother squawking at Woodcutter that they would go further and deeper into the woods the next day.

When everyone was sleeping, Hansel and Gretel sneaked out of bed to gather more pebbles. But Stepmother had locked the door and windows. They could not leave the house! They sadly went back to bed.

The next morning, Stepmother again gave Hansel and Gretel a half loaf of bread. They again set out for the woods, but this time they took a different path through the woods, one much less traveled.

Hansel did not have pebbles to mark the path. He took out the bread and strewed a small piece of bread every twenty steps or so. They walked for a long time. Finally, Stepmother told Hansel and Gretel to sit and rest while they went to look for berries and other fruit.

Again, the children sat and waited. They nibbled on what was left of the bread. The sun was nearly at the end of its daily orbit. Shadows grew longer and longer. The woods grew darker and darker. Stars started to come out and twinkle. Gretel signed to Hansel, "They are not coming back."

Hansel replied, "I agree. Let's go home."

They got up and started to follow the path of the tiny pieces of bread—but the tiny pieces of bread were gone! The birds had eaten them! How would they get home?

Hansel kept a cool head. "Come, Gretel, we will find our way back." They walked and walked along the path, but it had many forks. They had to decide which fork to take, and they walked and walked for a long time. Finally they had to admit they were lost. The woods were dark and dense. It was hard for the moonlight to shine through. They could not see the stars above anymore to help guide them home. They were exhausted and no longer knew which way to turn. They found an area covered with soft moss, and they lay down to go to sleep for the night. The next morning, they would be able to see better and would find their way home.

Morning came. Sunshine made its way through the tall tree tops and lit the underbelly of the forest in wavering dapples of simmering light. The shadows of the sun flickering through

the leaves woke Hansel and Gretel. They rubbed their eyes, wearily got up, and started to walk again. The path got narrower and narrower and then disappeared altogether. They neared a clearing in the woods, and saw a cottage.

As they got nearer the cottage, they saw that it was made entirely of cookies and candy! They were so hungry they lost no time tearing small pieces off the cottage and eating the goodies. Suddenly a little old lady came out of the cottage, saw that they were famished, and invited them in to eat. Hansel and Gretel happily accepted her invitation and went in the house. They realized that she could not see very well, so they came closer and signed more clearly, "Thank you! We are so glad to be here."

When the old lady saw that Hansel and Gretel signed, she exclaimed, "You are not allowed to sign! Signs are revolting, and sign language is outlawed everywhere. I convened a congress and we conjured a spell against signs. Ooooh, what a magnificent spell!"

She beckoned to the children and said, "Come and see." She led the children outside to look at the roof. Hansel and Gretel were horrified to see that the roof was covered with children's hands, cut off at the wrist. Each hand had been dipped in crystal candy of different colors before being nailed on the roof. They realized that the old lady was a witch who enticed Deaf children to come in to kill them and use their hands as shingles on the roof.

Suddenly Witch's clammy and bony hand clamped Hansel's wrist and she yanked him back into the house. Hansel struggled but could not break loose. Witch pushed Hansel into a cage and locked the door. Gretel started to cry, and Witch shushed her with the warning that she would beat Hansel if Gretel did not stop crying. She then made Gretel cook, clean, wash, sew, sweep and do as she was ordered, from morning to night. Otherwise, she said, she would beat and eat Hansel.

Every day Witch fed Hansel well, to fatten him up. Every day Witch asked Hansel to stick his hand out of the cage so Witch could feel it since she could not see it very well. Every day

Hansel held out a chicken bone for her to feel. Every day Witch cried in despair, "Not fat enough. Eat more!"

There was a bald patch on the roof that leaked when it rained, and on the floor was a pot to catch the leaks. The roof needed two more pairs of hands to close the gap. Finally after weeks of feeding Hansel and noting no improvement in the growth of his hands, Witch lost her patience. "No matter, the time has come for your hands to become shingles." She told Gretel to start a fire under a huge kettle; when the water was hot enough, Hansel would be thrown into it. Witch told Gretel to go up the stepladder to the edge of the pot and see if the water was boiling.

Gretel whimpered, "But I do not know how to do that."

"Just go up the steps and see if the water is boiling."

"I don't know how. Why don't you show me how?"

"You good-for-nothing wretch!" screeched Witch. "I'll do it!"

Witch climbed up the steps to check the water, and as she got nearer the top, Gretel pushed her in and Witch shattered into tiny shards of glass inside the pot.

Gretel got out the key, unlocked the cage, and let Hansel out. They hugged and cried and laughed now that they were free. They searched the house and found a gold compass that would help lead them home. They also found a treasure chest full of gold coins and notes of praise from ear horn companies around the world.

They stuffed their pockets and knapsacks with the gold coins and used the compass to guide them home.

After three days of walking in the woods, they finally arrived home.

Woodcutter was sitting alone at the table, mournfully staring at a photo of Hansel and Gretel.

"Dad, Dad!" Hansel and Gretel shouted and jumped on him.

"Hansel and Gretel!" Woodcutter cried happily. "What a relief! My heart broke when you left and did not return."

They embraced each other tightly.

"Look, Dad, we killed the big, bad Witch and we took her money. Life will be better now," Hansel said.

"Where is Stepmother?" Gretel asked.

"She had a heart attack three days ago and died," responded Woodcutter. He didn't look too sad. He showed them a newsprint flyer proclaiming the end of the sign language prohibition.

The family lived happily ever after.

THE ANT AND THE GRASSHOPPER

 grasshopper was hopping happily in the meadow one beautiful summer day. The sky was blue, with nary a cloud, and trees swayed in the gentle breeze. Wild, colorful flowers sprouted everywhere. Grasshopper wanted this day to last forever, but he knew that before too long, it would be September. School would start in September. Grasshopper did not care about getting ready for school. There would be plenty of time to catch up on that—later!

As he hopped, Grasshopper spied his two ant friends sitting under a tree, reading a book and talking and signing to each other about the book.

"What are you doing?" asked Grasshopper.

"We are working on our reading skills," responded Alexandra Ant. Anthony Ant nodded in agreement.

Grasshopper doubled up in laughter. "Silly! It's a beautiful day. Why not come and play with me instead?"

"No, we want to be ready for kindergarten when school starts. We want to be able to read and be skilled in both the written word and the signed word," Anthony said.

"Oh, that's easy to do," chuckled Grasshopper. "Why bother with that? You can always catch up later. That is what school is for."

The ants were adamant, though. They wanted to have the skills so they could do well in school. Alexandra shook her head and said, "No, you go ahead and play. We're enjoying learning how to read and sign. This is really fun."

"Suit yourselves," Grasshopper shrugged. "See you next month in school," said Grasshopper as he merrily hopped away.

The waning days of summer soon transformed the trees into a canvas of brilliant autumn colors. September arrived all too soon, which meant it was time to attend school. Insects trekked to school. Grasshopper spotted Alexandra and Anthony Ant in his classroom. Their eyes were bright and they were eager to start school. Grasshopper rolled his eyes and said, "Big deal. This class will be easy."

Teacher Spider sat on a chair at the head of class. He welcomed the class, all eight of his arms waving as he signed. "Welcome to Progressive School. We will follow standards of expectations for behavior and for academic achievement. We will start with an assessment of your knowledge and your reading skills." He passed out test books and pencils and the pupils started writing in the test books. Grasshopper stared at his test book in disbelief. He did not understand anything! He did not even know if the book was upside down. He saw that Alexandra and Anthony Ant were busily and happily scribbling away in the test books. He began to panic.

At the end of the class, the test books were all turned in to Teacher Spider. He announced, "Those of you who have done well will have increased recess time. Those who did not do well must stay during recess daily and catch up."

Grasshopper groaned and slumped in his chair as he watched his friends play outside during recess. He was stuck inside, catching up. Now he understood his folly.

MORAL: Success depends on being ready for school.

BEAUTY AND THE BEAST

n a town way yonder, there lived a wealthy shopkeeper who was blessed with three daughters, Beatrice, Bernice, and Beauty. One day the shopkeeper needed to go to a far-away country to purchase goods for his store. Before he left, he asked his daughters what they wanted him to bring back from his journey. Beatrice asked for an exotic dress. Bernice asked for an extraordinary shawl. Beauty, the youngest daughter, asked in halting speech, "Nothing, dear Father. Just an exquisite red rose."

"Speak more clearly," Father said, "I can't understand you."

"Just a red rose," repeated Beauty, struggling to pronounce the "r."

Father hugged his daughters, and gave Beauty one more special hug.

"Fortunately," thought Father to himself as he rode away, "Beauty is smart, with exemplary skills in reading and writing," Beauty was Deaf and had been practicing her speech ever since she was a little toddler. Her intelligence, warm personality, trustworthiness, and sunny outlook on life made her the apple of his eye.

Three weeks later, Father started on his journey back home. The bridge across a raging river had been washed away by heavy rainstorms. So he had to take a detour through a deep forest, on a path very rarely traveled. The path zigzagged through the dark, dense forest. The detour took so long that the sun set.

Father was a good navigator and was skilled in using the North Star to guide him. But ominous clouds blanketed the sky. Finally, weary and chilled to the bone, Father espied a strange castle. He decided to head for it and seek shelter for the evening.

As Father neared the castle, he noticed that it was bordered by an intricate wrought iron fence. He tried the giant gates and was relieved to find they were not locked. He rode his horse along the wide, finely manicured lane leading to the castle. He tied the horse up near the front door, took the bridle off, and put a warm blanket over the horse.

Father then knocked at the door, but there was no answer. He turned the knob and the door swung open. He entered the massive hallway and walked gingerly to one of the rooms. To his astonishment, there was a roaring fire in the dining room, and plenty of food on the dining room table. Father called out, "Is anyone here?" several times before he gave up, sat down at the table, and ate heartily. He went to sit in an easy chair next to the fireplace, put his feet up on the ottoman, and fell fast asleep.

The next morning, rays of sunshine peeked through the opening in the heavy velvet curtains and woke Father up. He looked around the room but could see no sign of life. It was time for him to leave anyway, so he decided to depart without further ado. He fed his horse and got it ready for the last leg of the trip home. There were gorgeous red rose bushes on both sides of the entrance door. Remembering his promise to Beauty to bring home an exquisite red rose, he plucked one and carefully put it in his coat buttonhole.

Just before he mounted his horse, he heard a ferocious roar.

"You come in my castle, eat my food, sleep in my chair and now you steal my rose!?" snarled Beast.

Father turned around to look and was terrified to see such a horrific creature. Although elegantly dressed in a velvet cape, silk shirt, leather trousers and knee high boots, Beast had the face of a lion, his face framed by a shaggy tawny mane. His mouth was shut, but his four canine teeth sticking out of both sides of his mouth gleamed. Claw-tipped paws showed at the end of his shirt sleeves.

Father fell to his knees and begged Beast for mercy. He shakily explained that he had plucked this rose for his daughter Beauty, who only wanted a rose. His voice and hands were trembling.

Beast growled through clenched teeth, "I will let you go only if you promise to send Beauty here to live with me."

Father was so frightened out of his mind that he readily agreed, hastily mounted his horse and raced out of the gates.

All the way home, Father cried, wrung his hands, and lamented, "Oh what have I done?!"

Upon arrival, Father was greeted by his three daughters—who were alarmed to see how terrible Father looked.

"What's wrong, Father? Are you sick?" they asked.

Father cried, wrung his hands, and repeated, "Oh what have I done?!"

"What?" they asked.

Father shared his encounter at the strange castle and how Beast was ready to pounce upon him for stealing a rose, unless he promised to send Beauty to Beast. "No, I'd rather die than to do that," he wailed. He wrote on a chalkboard to tell Beauty, who had been trying to understand the conversation with concern.

"No, Father," Beauty responded, with a look of steel in her eyes and her jaw set, "I love you so much. I will honor your promise. I will go."

"No, Beauty. What about your speech lessons?" Father grabbed an excuse out of thin air, not willing to see his beloved Beauty sacrificed to Beast.

A sly smile crossed Beauty's face, "I'm sorry, Father, but to tell you the truth, Teacher and I just play card games with tarot decks for the full hour instead of practicing speech. Speech lessons don't help me. I'll pack up and leave first thing in the morning."

After breakfast, amidst much wailing and hugging by Father and her sisters, Beauty mounted her favorite horse and departed, anxious yet determined to uphold her family's honor and dignity.

After a few hours of riding, Beauty arrived at the castle and peered through the iron gates. The majestic castle, made out of grey stone blocks, stood tall and proud. It had stained glass windows. Its turrets and steeples rose high in the sky. On its pennants was the owner's coat of arms: a large blue paw outlined in yellow. The gardens surrounding the castle were filled with lush rosebushes and azaleas, all in gorgeous bloom. Luscious orange blossoms and honeysuckles perfumed the air.

As she took in the scenery, the front gates suddenly opened. Beauty's heart pounded as she rode her horse along the long path up to the front door. Dismounting, she tied her horse up near the front door, and shakily climbed a few steps to the front door. She thought it odd that nobody greeted her at the door, not even a valet. As she reached out, the door swung open. She gasped, but there was nobody there.

Beauty entered the massive hallway and the door slammed so hard behind her that she could feel its vibrations. She noticed that candelabras along the hallway walls were facing her. As she walked down the hallway, the candelabras aligned with her, lit up, and swung in her direction. She looked back, and the candelabras still faced her, although the lights slowly dimmed. It seemed the candelabras had eyes that followed her.

Beauty entered the parlor and marveled at the loveliness of the room. It was filled with fine furniture and paintings. The dark mahogany furniture had carved lion's feet. There was a roaring fire in the fireplace, framed with Delft tiles and topped with a carved mahogany wood mantle. Between two armchairs, there was a serving table with a glossy top that softly lit up. She looked around the room, and her heart nearly stopped when she spotted a creature sitting in the armchair, facing the tall stained glass windows on the other side of the room.

It was inevitable that she would meet Beast. She carefully tiptoed to the front of the chair and peered at the creature. Quivering, she forced herself to curtsey to Beast and spoke haltingly, "I'm Beauty. Father sent me."

Beast looked up at Beauty from his seat. He could understand her even though her speech was not clear. She was indeed ravishingly gorgeous, even if she was trembling. She was too scared to look at Beast in the eye, instead averting her eyes to his tailored suit and shirt embellished with lace.

Beast stood up and bowed, and tried to compensate for his ferocious looks by signing gently, "Welcome to my castle and my home. It is now your home too."

Beauty was shaking with fear, yet she was mesmerized by Beast's hand movements and the kind look in his eyes.

"I'll show you to your room," Beast signed as he led her through the hallway, lined with the same candelabras with eyes and arms that seemed to follow them. The lights brightened as they approached, and dimmed after they passed. Beast gave her the biggest and finest bedroom in the castle. The windows faced the gardens and fountain outdoors. Around the gushing fountain was a clipped path, lined with yellow and blue pansies. The room faced south so it was sunny and warm. The furniture and bed were equally exquisite and looked very comfortable.

"You should find everything you need in this room. Dinner will be served at 6:00 p.m. in the dining room," Beast signed, bowing and leaving Beauty alone in the room.

Beauty's head was spinning. Beast's savage looks belied his apparently gentle, civilized nature. And he moved his hands to talk with her! She replayed his signs again and again in her head, not quite understanding what he had signed, yet understanding the message. It was clear to her that he had said he welcomed her into his home and that it was her home, too. He also cared enough to make her feel at home by giving her a beautiful bedroom. The bedspread was exotic with golden and silver threads interwoven into rainbows of colors. On the dressing table were a golden hairbrush and comb, and vials of perfumes and small vases filled with flowers. The closet was full of lovely gowns and shoes. Yet she still was anxious.

Beauty was on time for dinner and found Beast sitting at the opposite end of a long table. The room was lit by a chandelier that brightened as she entered the room. The table glowed warmly with more light as she sat down, and she could see Beast easily. There were fragrant flowers in vases on the table, low enough to not obstruct sightlines. The food was delicious. Neither talked during dinner. After dinner, Beauty excused herself and went back to her room under the watchful eyes of the candelabras. She opened her window and let the moonlight in, and took a deep breath. She watched the dancing fountain in the garden and marveled at the changing rainbow colors of the waters as they rose and fell, magically and rhythmically. It seemed like hours later that Beauty fell asleep.

Days passed. Beast was always kind to Beauty. He let her roam around most of the enormous castle, but a few doors were always closed. He let her wander around the beautiful garden within the boundaries of the iron fence. Sometimes they went horseback riding around the expansive property. As they walked or rode, Beast chatted with Beauty in gestures and sign language, slowly at first and then at almost a natural conversational rate. On some days, Beauty sat in the parlor, crocheting lace or painting pictures. She sat at a table that glowed, helping her see the lace or paint better. Beast kept her company, sitting near her and reading one of his many books from his library. Sometimes he would call out holograms from the books and they watched the avatars narrate stories in sign language. Beauty had come to expect the unexpected in this enchanted castle.

Beauty's fear of Beast started to melt away, and she began to consider him a friend.

"Are you Deaf, too?" Beauty asked Beast one day.

"Of course, why?" responded Beast.

"You have so much knowledge, experience, and skills for a Deaf person," Beauty remarked.

"Beauty, Deaf people can do anything, and you can, too," Beast answered tenderly.

Beauty enjoyed chatting with Beast and she marveled at how easy it was to use sign language and how profound their discourses were. She began to look forward to their conversations as her mastery of sign language improved. They talked about everything under the sun as they shared meals or walks in the gardens, or as they sat in the parlor talking into the wee hours of the morning.

One day Beauty shared with Beast that she missed her father and sisters very much and wondered how they were doing. Worrying about them made her sad. Beast offered her an elaborate golden hand mirror, and when Beauty looked at it, she was startled to see Father's image in it. She could see her father going about his life, and felt reassured that he was all right.

Another day, Beast invited Beauty to visit his music room. Beauty looked at Beast with an incredulous look on her face. "Music? We can't hear." Beauty remembered the hours of boredom that she endured as she sat through music recitals at home with Father playing the fiddle, Beatrice pounding on the piano keys, and Bernice stroking a harp. Beauty was given a small pair of cymbals and was told when to clap them, following the rhythm of their playing. She felt like a wind-up tin monkey clapping cymbals. She usually tried to find a reason to excuse herself from these recitals.

"Come and see," Beast beckoned her as he led her through the hallway to a special music room.

As they entered, soft lights from above glowed. There were hundreds of strange glass bulbs and tubes on the wall. Along the ceiling there were strands of transparent ribbons. On the floor were tall crystals of various shapes and colors.

Beast and Beauty sat down at a bench next to a table with a mirror on the top. "Here we go again," thought Beauty as she braced herself for another boring bout of senseless music.

Beast waved his hands over the table, and suddenly the room burst into rhythmic glows as the bulbs and tubes changed colors and patterns in tune with Beast's hand movements across the mirrored table. Colors glowed, flowed, and ebbed. The ribbons above fluttered in clusters of colors and waves. The crystals gleamed, and tiny bubbles of air danced in them. The room was transformed into a symphony of colors and rhythms. Images of dandelions in a swaying meadow, ocean waves pounding on the shores, and rustling leaves on trees appeared at different times and places in the room, showcasing nature's visual musicality. Sometimes words or poetic phrases flashed across the room. The bench softly vibrated according to the tunes.

Beauty had never seen anything like that in her life. Putting her hand on Father's fiddle as he played did not invoke anything near the same emotions that the visual music did.

"Music is not about hearing. Music is in the heart," said Beast. "Joys and sorrows of the heart are conveyed and transformed and intertwined into connections of all kinds."

Beauty sat enraptured as Beast played songs from famous poets that she had read about, as well as those he had composed himself. She could understand them and she was deeply stirred by them. As he played, sometimes the lights were soft, warm and soothing, like ripples of water on a golden pond and gentle breezes rustling the meadow grasses. Sometimes the lights simmered, sizzled, flashed, and rocked across a range of sensations from quiet to loud, from soft to bold, from soothing to booming. They evoked the changing of clouds as they crossed the sky, lightning during a midnight sky, the soothing sing-song of a sewing machine, a mother's gentle stroking of her baby's hair, the bubbling of a soup on the stove, the passing of rows of trees through the woods, the cyclical crash of waves on the shore, the whirling of leaves from trees during a storm.

Beauty was astonished, overcome with emotion, and moved to tears by the magnificent musical display of visual sensations and images. Words were not needed.

Beast looked at Beauty. Finally he broke the long silence by saying, "Would you like to try your hand at creating music?"

"Yes, please teach me how!"

Beast put her hand in his paw to guide her. Beauty was amazed at how soft and furry his paw was, almost like the fur of a kitten. The softness belied the look of the strong large paw. They played on, experimenting with different hues, shades, volumes and patterns of light.

After a while, Beast said, "Let's sit back and let the music play itself." He turned on a switch on the side of the table, turned on its memory bank, and selected the songs they had just created. The room reverberated repeatedly with dancing colors, images and words. Beauty sat enthralled as Beast put his arm around her. She fit perfectly in the crook of his arm. Warm feelings washed over her as she sat there, taking in the visual symphony and the closeness of Beast.

At dinner that evening, Beast asked Beauty to marry him.

Beauty's eyes widened with surprise. She had come to like Beast dearly, but she could not imagine marrying him! "Oh Beast, I do like you, but I can't marry you," she demurred. "We are so different."

"No, we are truly more alike than we are different," responded Beast with a sad look in his eyes, "but I understand."

Days at the castle passed by idyllically. Days were spent walking around the garden, arranging flowers, riding, sewing, reading, painting, reading or watching stories, creating music, and engaging in stimulating conversations.

One day Beauty looked at her magic mirror to check on Father and was shocked to see him in bed, looking stricken. He looked like he might die.

"Beast, I need to go home. Father may die. Please let me go," Beauty pleaded.

"Absolutely not! You promised to stay here with me forever," Beast snapped.

Beauty ran, crying, to her room.

Beast also had tears in his eyes, but he was not willing to let go of Beauty. Once she left, she might never return.

At dinnertime, Beast had a change of heart and said, "Beauty, you may go home but only for seven days." Beauty's heart jumped with relief and joy as she promised him that she would return in a week.

When Father saw Beauty, he immediately cheered up and quickly began to recover. Beauty loved being with Father and her two sisters, although she missed the interesting conversations and experiences at the castle. She realized she was very happy at the castle. Days passed. Beauty forgot about her promise to return in seven days.

One day she remembered the golden magic mirror that she had brought with her from the castle. She wanted to show it to Father and her sisters. She looked at the mirror and was shocked to see Beast crumpled on the floor in the castle. He was ill and dying, signing as he cried, "Beauty, please come back. I need you. I love you."

Beauty's heart sank. She had never meant to hurt Beast. She explained to Father and her sisters that she had to return to Beast at the castle, hugged them and bid them farewell.

As soon as she arrived at the castle, she raced through the massive hallways, looking for him. He was nowhere to be found. She took the magic mirror out of her purse and saw Beast withering in agony on the floor, but which room? She used the mirror to lead her through the maze of hallways to the room where Beast lay.

The door was closed, but it swung open when Beauty arrived. She rushed to him and knelt beside him. "Please don't die. I will stay here forever with you," sobbed Beauty as she cradled Beast in her arms.

The room felt strange. Beauty looked around. She had never been in this room, which was filled with mirrors from floor to ceiling on the walls all around the room. There seemed to be ghosts in the mirrors watching them.

Beauty's tears fell on Beast's eyes. Beast's eyes slowly opened. "My Beauty, you've come back!" he moaned. "I am dying. My family has come to bid me farewell," he said, pointing to the apparitions in the mirrors, which gradually transformed into weeping creatures who looked like Beast.

"No! I love you. Don't die. I want to be with you forever!" Beauty sobbed and kissed him as she held him tightly.

With those words, Beast miraculously stood up with a happy look. He picked up Beauty, swung her around, and said, "I was under a curse and only your true love could break the spell. I have been waiting here in this castle for years for you!"

Beauty was astonished. "What do you mean?"

Beast explained that he was from a planet called Eyeth in another galaxy. He had been banished to Earth under a curse by a witch from the planet Heinicketh. He was doomed to die on Earth unless an Earthling truly loved him, breaking the spell.

"Eyeth?" asked Beauty.

"Yes," Beast responded, "Eyeth is where I am from. On Eyeth, there is equality, full access, social justice and love for all creatures. Everyone signs there, and I know you will love living there."

He then got down on his knee and signed tenderly, "Will you marry me?" Beauty gasped and began crying with joy.

Beast continued, "We will be transported back to Eyeth, and I know you will love it there. If you marry me, your appearance will be transformed and you will look like me."

"Beauty is in the eyes of the beholder." Beauty happily said. "Yes, yes, I will marry you!"

As she said yes, she could feel her appearance already changing. Her vision became very sharp and she could see 360 degrees around the room without having to swivel her head. Her sense of smell was heightened and she could smell the scent of the roses outside. Her sense of touch became sensitive and the sensation of holding Beast's furry paw sent tingles all over her. Soft downy fur covered her body. She felt like she could almost read Beast's mind and anticipate his feelings. She shared his sensation of pure happiness.

The creatures in the mirror cheered, waved their paws, and faded away.

Beast said, "Come now. It is time for us to go to Eyeth, sweet Eyeth."

On Eyeth, they were married and lived happily ever after.

PHOENIX

t was late one afternoon on a rainy day at Grandma's house. Little Alice asked Grandma, "Please tell me a story."

Grandma pointed to her collection of books and answered, "Certainly. Which one of these books would you like for me to read to you?"

"No," signed Alice emphatically, "tell me a new story."

Grandma thought for a while and her wrinkled face lit up. "Have you heard of the Phoenix bird?"

"No!" responded Alice with delight. "Do tell me!"

They sat down in a large, cozy armchair in front of a flickering fireplace, with Alice sitting on the arm of the chair, facing Grandma.

"This is a story about our people," started Grandma, "and of courage, resilience and persistence." She began telling the story.

Once upon a time in the Garden of Eden, there lived a bird, Phoenix. It was the most beautiful bird on earth. Its feathers were brilliant shades of the setting sun, ranging from yellow to crimson, highlighted at the ends with the colors of a rainbow. Wherever the bird soared, amazing rainbow beams followed.

When Adam and Eve were banished from the Garden of Eden, sparks from a flaming bolt of lightning that came down from heaven hit Phoenix's nest, which burst into flames. Phoenix

perished in the flames. But within the nest, there was one red egg, which hatched and another Phoenix emerged.

You see, good things come after something bad happens. Sunshine comes after each rainstorm. Every hundred years or so, something happens and Phoenix burns itself to death in its nest, but each time, a new Phoenix, the only one in the world, emerges from the red egg and soars.

For thousands of years, Deaf people were not considered worthy members of society. They were left to fend for themselves without education and jobs. In 360 BC, Socrates stated that Deaf people were incapable of language and ideas. In 355 BC, Aristotle said, "Those who were born Deaf all become senseless and incapable of reason."

Phoenix shuddered and went into a deep sleep.

The world did not see Phoenix again until 1520, when a Spanish monk, Pedro Ponce de Leon, developed one of the first manual alphabets while working with Deaf children of wealthy aristocrats. de Leon was the first teacher for Deaf children anywhere, and established a school for Deaf students at the San Salvador Monastery in Oña. Ponce de Leon's work demonstrated that Deaf people were capable of learning.

Phoenix opened one eye.

Spanish priest Juan Pablo Bonet pioneered education for several Deaf children from royal families in Spain. Literacy was a requirement for legal recognition as an heir, so royal families wanted their Deaf children to be educated. Bonet published the first book on sign language and education of Deaf children in 1620. His published system of signs and manual alphabet became the basis for sign languages in Spain, France, and later the United States.

Phoenix opened the other eye.

Around 1690, approximately 200 settlers on Martha's Vineyard in Massachusetts came from Kent and Sussex Counties in England.

They carried genes leading to different levels of hearing, and 1 in 155 of those settlers bore Deaf children. They formed their own sign language, and everyone on the island signed with each other. Deaf and hearing people married each other, had good jobs, and were treated equally.

Phoenix sprung to life!

In 1760, French priest Abbé de l'Épée dedicated himself to the instruction of Deaf children, and established the first free public school in the world for Deaf pupils, the Nationale des Sourds-Muets, in Paris. Deaf people, if they could read and write, could receive religious sacraments and avoid going to hell. His "Signed French" system of instruction was built on the natural French Sign Language used by the Deaf community. His public advocacy and methodical instruction helped Deaf people succeed in schools, gain employment, and defend themselves in court for the first time.

Phoenix soared!

In 1815, in the United States, Thomas Hopkins Gallaudet met a young Deaf girl, Alice Cogswell. Gallaudet was upset that there was no school program for her. He sailed to London in search of an educational method to teach Alice and others like her. However, the school in London was a private oral school and refused to share its secrets with Gallaudet. He then journeyed to Paris and visited the Institut National de Jeunes Sourds de Paris, where he met an exemplary Deaf teacher, Laurent Clerc. Studying three months at the Institute, Gallaudet was impressed with Clerc and realized that successful programs needed Deaf leaders and educators. During their 52-day voyage across the Atlantic Ocean to the United States in 1816, Gallaudet and Clerc taught each other English and sign language. Upon arrival in Hartford, Connecticut, they founded the first school for Deaf students in the United States, the American School for the Deaf, in 1817. Education in the United States with sign language might have never happened without the partnership between Clerc and Gallaudet.

Phoenix soared again!

In 1857, Thomas Gallaudet's son, Edward Miner Gallaudet, helped establish the Columbia Institution for the Instruction of the Deaf and Dumb and the Blind for Deaf children and orphans. It expanded into a college program, and in 1864, during the Civil War, the U.S. Congress authorized the institute to confer college degrees, with President Abraham Lincoln signing the bill into law. The National Deaf-Mute College, now known as Gallaudet University, was the first college in the world established for Deaf students and is still the only university in the world primarily for Deaf students. The college produced many Deaf graduates and leaders who went forth and established schools and programs all over the country and world.

Phoenix soared again!

The world plunged into darkness in 1880, when the International Congress of the Educators of the Deaf (ICED) met in Milan, Italy in 1880 and passed a resolution to ban sign language in the education of Deaf students and to discourage the employment of Deaf teachers. The National Association of the Deaf (NAD) was established that same year, and continues as the world's first continuous advocacy organization of, by, for and with Deaf people, to promote social justice, human rights, equality and quality of life for all.

Phoenix soared again!

George Veditz, born to German immigrants in Maryland, was fluent in American Sign Language, English, and German. He attended the Maryland School for the Deaf and Gallaudet University. In 1904, he was elected president of the NAD, and his primary focus was the protection, preservation and promotion of sign language. Sign language at the time was threatened by the global spread of oralism as a result of the 1880 Milan resolution. Silent films became popular in the 1910s, and in 1913, Veditz led the NAD's efforts in fundraising, filming notable signers and advocating for the beauty and value of signs to be preserved for all of mankind. These films became the first anywhere to record sign language and are currently in the National Film Registry at the Library of Congress. Among his many notable quotes are, "As long as we have Deaf people on earth, we will have signs.

And as long as we have our films, we can preserve signs in their old purity. It is my hope that we will all love and guard our beautiful sign language as the noblest gift God has given to Deaf people."

Phoenix soared again!

The *Silent Worker* newspaper started in 1888 and was published monthly by the New Jersey School for the Deaf. In the 1920s and 1930s, Deaf people faced many issues: eugenics, suppression of sign language, the sharp decrease in Deaf teachers, a ban on the use of sign language in schools, a Congressional proposal to ban marriage among Deaf people, a proposed ban on Deaf automobile drivers, a struggle for employment, and much more. The *Silent Worker* contained articles and editorials by Deaf authors about sign language, education, employment and civil rights. As the influence of the Milan resolution banning sign language spread, the *Silent News* served as a beacon of information, light, and hope for the Deaf community. However, in 1929, the New Jersey school administration ceased publishing the *Silent Worker* and dismissed its editor, George Porter. Underground newspapers were started. Finally, the NAD published a new edition of the *Silent Worker* in 1948. The *Silent Worker*, later renamed *The Deaf American,* continued for years.

Phoenix soared again!

When World War II broke out, thousands of men in the United States were called to serve as soldiers for their country. This left a huge void for workers in the United States, and created opportunities for women and Deaf people to prove themselves as very capable workers, ranging from riveters to supervisory jobs. As unfortunate as WWII was, it helped to open doors and showcase the ability of Deaf people.

Phoenix soared again!

In 1945, the United Nations was established in New York City to promote international cooperation after World War II. In 1951, the World Federation of the Deaf (WFD) was established, along the same values as the United Nations, with a focus on promoting sign language, sharing information, and strengthening advocacy networks with national associations of Deaf people. First established in Italy, the WFD currently is headquartered in Helsinki, Finland. Both the UN and the WFD share a logo and aim to enhance human rights for everyone.

Phoenix soared again!

Sign language was viewed by many as a deficient system of gestures, and shunned by those who believed it harmed Deaf children's acquisition of English. This view held steadfast for centuries, especially after the 1880 Congress banning sign language, until Dr. William Stokoe's research on sign language structure and linguistics resulted in two groundbreaking books, *Sign Language Structure* (1960) and *A Dictionary of American Sign Language (ASL) on Linguistic Principles* (1965). His research validated ASL as a language in and of itself, separate from English, and dramatically shifted world views about sign language users and their distinctive language, community and culture. Education of Deaf people started to once again include ASL along with English.

Phoenix soared again!

Deaf people, as members of a cultural minority, started to have pride in their language, culture, and community. Bernard Bragg was a pioneer in theater, as a mime who had a weekly television show, "The Quiet Man," from 1958 to 1961. He helped lay the groundwork for the development of Deaf theater as an art form, and co-founded the National Theatre of the Deaf (NTD) in 1967 when the U.S. Congress authorized its establishment. The NTD and later the Deaf West Theatre created careers for Deaf people as well as contributed to public awareness and appreciation for the many talents of Deaf people and the beauty of ASL. Thousands of audience members, hearing and Deaf, fell in love with the beauty of ASL, and thousands of classes and programs in ASL and Deaf Studies were offered. After the international Deaf Way festival at Gallaudet in 1989, Deaf View/Image Art (De'VIA) emerged as a genre as Deaf artists expressed the Deaf way of life through the arts. Poetry, written literature, and filmed stories in ASL flourished, contributing to a growing, respectable corpus of academic knowledge. The National Technical Institute for the Deaf at the Rochester Institute of Technology in Rochester, New York, and the Model Secondary School for the Deaf at Gallaudet were established around 1968. It was also during this era that Deaf people worked with sign language interpreters to establish professional interpreting standards.

Phoenix soared again!

In 1988, when the Gallaudet University search for a new president resulted in a vote by its board to appoint a hearing person over two qualified Deaf candidates, the Deaf President Now movement erupted. After seven days of protests, which reverberated around the world and were supported by masses of people from all walks of life, the board reversed its decision and appointed Dr. I. King Jordan as the first Deaf president of the university. The right to self-representation, self-determination and self-governance, of, for, by and with Deaf people became embedded in the American landscape This human rights movement also led to the passage of the Americans with Disabilities Act in 1990, landmark legislation expanding rights of people with disabilities to equal opportunities in education, employment and community.

Phoenix soared again!

In 2010, at the International Congress of Education of the Deaf in Vancouver, Canada, 600 participants signed a resolution repudiating the destructive 1880 Milan resolution against sign language and Deaf teachers. The unifying message of the diverse plenary speakers during this Congress was the importance of sign language, culture, and community for all Deaf children. This significant action embraced the New Era guiding principles reinforcing human rights and alliances in education.

Phoenix soared again!

After decades of limitations caused by Alexander Bell's invention of the telephone, the advent of technology transformed telephones from a bane to a boon. Teletypewriters (TTYs) hooked up to telephones enabled Deaf people to independently call each other using text and to use relay services to contact parties that did not have TTYs. Television shows and films were captioned. A significant breakthrough occurred when the quality of pictures on videophones and handheld devices finally allowed clear video conversations, either point-to-point or through sign-interpreted relay services. Deaf children could also use video relay services to communicate with non-signing family members.

Phoenix soared again!

Grandma smiled and gazed at Alice, who had sat mesmerized throughout her story. "Can you think of another example of when Phoenix lives again, dear granddaughter?"

Alice furrowed her brows, thought for a minute, and answered. "I know! A mother and her baby look at each other in the eyes, and the mother signs. The baby's eyes light up. Phoenix soars again!"

Grandma smiled, her eyes crinkling up and her face showing countless laugh lines. She stroked Alice's face gently with the back of her fingers, and slowly nodded.

"Yes, Phoenix soars again!"

ABOUT THE CONTRIBUTORS

Dr. Roslyn "Roz" Rosen was born to a Deaf family in the Bronx. She attended the Lexington School for the Deaf and Gallaudet University, where she met her husband and lifelong partner, Herb Rosen. Currently retired, her career has included being a rehabilitation counselor, Gallaudet University faculty, dean, and vice president of academic affairs at Gallaudet University, and director of the National Center on Deafness at California State University, Northridge. She is a past president of the National Association of the Deaf and a board member of the World Federation of the Deaf.

This is Roz's first book, but she has authored chapters in various books, such as *1776: Deaf People's Contribution*, *The Sands of Time: NAD Presidents 1880-2003*, and *ISMs, Identities and Intersectionality: Implications and Inclusion*, among others. She also has written numerous articles and provided numerous presentations on human rights, education, organizational development and leadership. Currently, Roz serves on the core team of Language Equality and Acquisition for Deaf Kids – Kindergarten Ready (LEAD-K), a national campaign to stop language deprivation. She also is a board member of the West Virginia School for the Deaf and Blind, and board member of Discovering Deaf Worlds. In her spare time, Roz strolls along beaches and dabbles in the arts. She and her husband have three children and nine grandchildren.

 **Yiqiao Wang** was born in Beijing, China, and came to the United States to pursue her studies. She has a bachelor's degree in digital media from Gallaudet University, and a master's degree in illustration from Savannah College of Art and Design. She is an artist-in-residence at the Motion Light Lab for the Visual Language and Visual Learning Center at Gallaudet University. Her other work includes being the illustrator for VL2's storybook apps, *The Baobab*, *The Blue Lobster*, and *The Solar System*. An adjunct faculty, she has also been invited to display her creations in art galleries and shows in Washington D.C., and at Rochester Institute of Technology.

 **Suzy Rosen Singleton** is the Chief of the Disability Rights Office of the Federal Communications Commission, and has practiced with the Commission since 2012. Her legal career started in 1992, and involved civil rights litigation for the now defunct California Center for Law and the Deaf, and disability policy work in the following former capacities: as the counsel for government affairs for the National Association of the Deaf, a special education law compliance officer for the U.S. Department of Education, and the ombuds for Gallaudet University. Suzy is licensed to practice in the District of Columbia, and holds a Juris Doctor from the UCLA School of Law, and a bachelor's degree in political science from the University of California, Berkeley. Cooking, reading, hiking, and sharing in laughter with dear friends and family are Suzy's favorite pastimes.